Tee Time

TRAGEDY

at the

SNOWY

PLOVER INN

Deanna Nese

Books in the Snowy Plover Inn series

Christmas at the Snowy Plover Inn (a novella)
Checked Out at the Snowy Plover Inn
Tee Time Tragedy at the Snowy Plover Inn

Visit deannanese.com

Tee Time
TRAGEDY
at the
SNOWY
PLOVER INN

Snowy Plover Inn Cozy Mysteries, Book 2

Deanna Nese

Secret Staircase Books

Tee Time Tragedy at the Snowy Plover Inn
Published by Secret Staircase Books, an imprint of
Columbine Publishing Group, LLC
PO Box 416, Angel Fire, NM 87710

Book layout and design by Secret Staircase Books
First e-book edition: March, 2026
First paperback edition: March, 2026
* * *

Publisher's Cataloging-in-Publication Data

Nese, Deanna.
Tee Time Tragedy at the Snowy Plover Inn / by Deanna Nese.
p. cm.
ISBN 978-1649142399 (paperback)
ISBN 978-1649142405 (e-book)

1. Snowy Plover Inn (Fictitious locale). 2. California coast—
Fiction. 3. Amateur sleuths—Fiction. 4. Women sleuths—Fiction. I.
Title
Snowy Plover Inn Cozy Mystery Series : Book 2.
Nese, Deanna., Snowy Plover Inn cozy mysteries.

BISAC : FICTION / Mystery & Detective.
813/.54

For my family …

Chapter 1

Sunday
Maxine

Max and Pearla couldn't resist a quick stop at Barnaby's, and though Max wasn't ready to admit it, a chance to see Tyne, the ruggedly handsome and charming owner. Smiling, he waved to them saying, "Your booth's open. Garlic fries?"

"Are we that predictable?" Pearla asked, as they settled into their usual comfy red vinyl booth to discuss the current and upcoming needs of the inn.

"Two raspberry iced teas?" Kelly called out from behind the bar. Pearla held a thumbs-up. It was too early for beer. Kelly delivered the iced teas, and a few minutes later, Tyne strode over. He was wearing his usual faded jeans and snug black t-shirt under a worn-in red plaid flannel. Leather flip-flops completed the look. He was an older version of a hipster, and Max felt her heart speed up as it always did in his presence. She smoothed down her dark blond, shoulder-length hair, wishing she'd thought to check her appearance before entering the restaurant.

"I'm glad you stopped in. I wanted to ask you something."

"Shoot," Pearla said.

"What're your opinions about the golf course? It's a sizeable piece of land. I'm sensing mixed feelings from the regulars," he said, while setting down a basket of Barnaby's signature fries.

Why does he always have to look so good? Max grabbed a fry and before depositing it directly into her mouth, responded, "It's shaping up. There's a lot of potential. Shame the family has to sell. I think it'll end up as a bidding war with the investors."

Tyne shoved into the booth next to Max while asking, "May I?"

"Sure," Pearla said. "We'd love to hear your thoughts, and everyone else's. You've always got the lowdown."

"Well, the timing's right. Once the Gateway Wellness Center opens, it should drive business; wives and girlfriends will hang out at the spa while the men golf. Then they'll stop here for some beers," Tyne said, grabbing three fries from the basket.

"Seriously Tyne? That's sexist. Who's to say men don't want spa treatments?" Max asked, nudging him and fixing him with a mock glare.

"And why are we assuming women don't golf?" Pearla added with a smirk. Both knew Tyne meant nothing by his remarks, it was just his way. He looked sheepish for a moment, finished chewing, and responded, "You're right. Just because I don't want a facial and a manicure, doesn't mean other men don't. I don't golf either," he said with a laugh. "Too boring."

"I didn't even know there was a golf course here when I first arrived. And I don't remember it from when I'd come to Silvermist as a kid. I suppose I never noticed," Max said.

"It was hidden in plain sight under all that overgrowth. Do we know why the owners let it go like that?" Pearla asked.

"Well, that land's been in the Worley family for generations, and for a while, maybe fifteen years ago, there was a thriving little nine-hole golf course. There were even a few small tournaments with semi-professionals. But, when the clubhouse burned down, none of the Worley kids wanted to rebuild. They put up a chain-link fence and some No Trespassing signs, then moved away and let it go. It's been an overgrown mess for years. It's only recently Pete Junior revived the first few holes, so investors can see the potential. The property is extensive enough for a full eighteen-hole course, and he and his brothers are motivated to sell. With the spa going in, they're seeing dollar signs," Tyne said, and added, "I'll bring out more fries. Didn't realize how hungry I was."

"That's okay. We're heading out in a few," Max said.

"Then these are on the house."

They watched him walk to the kitchen.

"*Silvermist Point of View* would've had something to say about the golf course. That writer had a knack for finding out all the juicy details," Pearla said, referring to the now-silenced village newsletter.

"Whether or not they were accurate," Max added, thinking about how desperate she'd felt when the gossip was untrue and aimed at the Snowy Plover Inn, and only months after she had taken over as the new owner. The little local newsletter had ceased with the death of Beth, all but confirming suspicions she wrote it.

Just then, Pearla put her finger to her lips and cocked her head toward the booth behind her. The booths' backs were tall, extending a foot above their heads, providing patrons with a sense of privacy. But if you listened carefully, you could be privy to the conversation of those behind you. Max fell silent and leaned across the table as they listened in. Two men were in a heated discussion.

"I don't like it, and I know Dad wouldn't either. That land should be sold to the conservancy. I told Pete that. I don't know what his angle is."

"Yeah, so that's not gonna happen, Bro. It's greed. A nice thought, but a non-profit will never pay what private investors can. Look at it this way, a small golf course is better than a real estate development with a bunch of cookie-cutter homes. Dad would have despised a planned neighborhood in Silvermist. He loved the character of the village."

"It's not even zoned for residential! The golf course is the only option Dad would be okay with. That, or donating it and taking a write-off. We could even call it Worley Park, or something like that, to honor his name."

"Look, we have to sell it. Pete will make sure we get the best possible price. We all need the money. Dad would understand; he'd never expect us to suffer financially."

"You're right. It might be a hard sell anyway, since it's not zoned for big development."

The other man let out a deep, sarcastic laugh. "Ha! Zoning laws can change. It just depends on who's got the cash. And the influence. But don't worry about it, Seth. Pete's taking care of it."

"That's what I'm afraid of. Just because he's the oldest, doesn't mean he's in charge."

"As the executor of Dad's will, he pretty much is."

The booth was too high for Max to get a decent look at the men. Kelly came over, they settled their check, and got up to leave. Max slid out of her seat in time to see the men exit out the back door.

"I don't recognize them," she said. "I don't think they're locals."

"Definitely not," Pearla agreed. "They must be Pete Worley's brothers."

* * *

The four potential investors would all be lodging at the Snowy Plover Inn. Pearla had taken the reservation from Pete Worley himself. Four upstairs rooms on either side of the central courtyard, all similar in size and amenities. Pete had requested the rooms be equal so as not to show favoritism to one prospective buyer over another. The investors would meet with the sellers to walk the course, see the town, and name their price. The highest bidder wins.

As the current hot topic of the town, the Worley property was the main focus of Thursday's residents' meeting. Every third Thursday, folks from Silvermist met in the living room of the inn. It was an informal gathering that often devolved into a gossip or gripe session, and last

Thursday speculation regarding the property abounded. Who would buy it, and what would that look like for the future of the town? Opinions were varied. Some were frustrated that it could be sold at all and would readily agree with the brother who wanted it donated to a conservancy. For a small faction of the town, any changes to the landscape of Silvermist Point were not welcome. They would stop time if they could to leave their little gem of Silvermist just as it had always been.

Chapter 2

Pearla

It had been two days since Pearla had strolled along the shoreline in front of the Snowy Plover Inn. Two days too many. *I need to feel the sand between my toes.* She fired off a quick message to Max before gathering her curly, chestnut-colored hair into a messy bun and securing it with a scrunchie.

Going for a shore stroll. I'll be back to set up reception

Pearla's daily beach walks were an addiction of the most favorable kind. If she'd heard about 'earthing' and 'grounding' before moving to Silvermist Point, she'd have scoffed and called it hippie nonsense. The healing properties of the ocean's rhythms, the salt air, and the invisible positive energy weren't easily explained. You had to immerse yourself to understand the peace it brought. In her previous life, her addiction was television, with occasional podcasts sprinkled in, and maybe a book or two a month—all forms of media tied to crime fiction. Watching, reading or listening to gruesome crimes play out, ideally in exotic and beautiful locations, oddly satisfied Pearla's need to experience beauty herself. Terrible things happen, even in beautiful places. *It's a good thing I stay home.*

The unexpected move to Silvermist Point was everything Pearla never knew she needed. Once again, she was so grateful to Max for offering her the opportunity to leave her job at the high school and help restore and manage the inn Max had bought on a whim. The Snowy Plover Inn was magical. Set back from the hauntingly misty shoreline, the original home was built in the style of a lighthouse, complete with a tower that provided a spectacular view.

Pearla's cozy studio was on the second floor above the reception area, and the back entrance opened onto the staircase of the tower, allowing her access to the circular glass room at the top any time she wanted. Her space had no walls except for the bathroom with its old-fashioned, cast-iron clawfoot tub. It was upon first seeing this tub that Pearla felt, deep in her bones, she had made the right move coming here. Silvermist Point was her place in the world.

She slid into flip-flops, grabbed the mesh bag she used to collect treasures, and slung it over her shoulder. The air was brisk, but not chilly. Pearla was confident last night's high tide would have left a bounty from the sea on the shoreline and hoped today's low tide might reveal even more. She exited through her back door and followed the spiral staircase down to the inner courtyard, then took the path leading through the inn's property to the trail down to the shore. The beach was not private, but to Pearla it felt that way as there were often no others in sight. Several other trails besides the one through the property led to the shoreline, but the ones from the upper cliffs were seldom used and were not well-maintained.

Pearla rushed into a shallow wave and reached down to grab the dime-sized piece of sea glass before it washed away. Red was the rarest color, but aqua was her favorite, along with deep blue. Her collection now almost filled a large-sized Mason jar, but included only one piece of yellow and a tiny shard of red. Most common were the whites and browns and greens, probably beer bottles in a former life. This was an aqua piece, beautifully seasoned. Pearla deemed it worthy of keeping and dropped it into her bag. She walked on.

Before she knew it, close to an hour had passed. The low tide created a path along the shore flanked by the cliffs on her left and the waves on her right. The path would narrow as the tide rose and eventually would disappear until the next low tide. *I'd better turn back.* As she reversed course, Pearla noticed a second set of footprints, heading the same way back. Someone must have taken one of the cliff trails down. Whomever these feet belonged to had high arches and a long stride.

For some steps, Pearla fit her own feet into the impressions. Then she strode along next to them until the prints disappeared by a second inlet leading to a trail connecting to the bluff above. She quickened her pace and arrived back at the inn with plenty of time to set up the afternoon wine and snacks in the living room.

Chapter 3

Maxine

Saturdays always felt like new beginnings. The inn's guests typically checked in on Saturdays and stayed the whole week. It had been the same when Max and Char would come as girls. Max thought Pete Worley had the right idea to book the rooms for the entire week. That way the potential investors could get a genuine feel for the area, and if all went well, the deal could be wrapped up during that time. Max was curious to meet the oldest Worley brother, whom she guessed was in charge.

"My brothers and I will lodge at our family's property," he'd told Pearla when he booked the rooms. Max had asked Tyne for the scoop on the brothers, but learned he didn't know much, only that the Worley family home was seldom used. It was a second home, and in recent years no one had seen much of the Worleys.

"You might ask the Trawls," Tyne suggested. "They've lived here forever."

Max had groaned at the proposition. "I wonder if I can get Larry or Colby to talk."

Conversation with the Trawls could best be described as tedious. Neither were social, to say the least, but since the attempted murder during the inn's grand opening, and their help in saving the inn's reputation, they had come to an understanding. Even Colby, who harbored childhood resentment of Max and her closest childhood friend, Char, was much more personable lately. He was working through the steps of Alcoholics Anonymous and had reached the one where he made amends.

Max found Larry and Colby on the path from the inn's property to the shore. Larry was wearing his typical uniform of overalls, a long-sleeved t-shirt and work boots. A bucket hat covered his thinning white hair. He was raking wood chips. Colby, sporting a worn-out Grateful Dead t-shirt and ripped jeans, was pulling weeds. Max carried a tote bag with a thermos of cold lemonade and three plastic glasses. She conjured up a cheerful smile as she approached.

"I brought you some lemonade." Max held up the bag.

Colby turned from his task, cocked an eyebrow, and ran a hand through his shaggy, overgrown hair. "What do you want?"

Hello to you, too.

"Colby!" Larry scolded his son.

"Sorry, I meant, 'Thank you'."

"Well, you're not wrong. I do want to ask you guys something. What do you know about the Worley family? Specifically, the brothers selling the land."

"They're dicks!" Colby shouted, no filter as usual.

"Can you elaborate?" Max asked, while calmly pouring him a lemonade.

"They were part of the vacation crowd. Always acted better than the local kids. We got into it a time or two. The sister was hot, though." And he made a lewd gesture.

Seriously? How old are you?

"Thanks for that. I didn't know they had a sister."

Larry took a long swig of his lemonade and said, "Annie. She's not been around. Didn't even come to her father's funeral. The whole town was there, even me. Poor Pete Senior. They didn't find him right away. The neighbor hadn't seen him, and when she went to check, well, he had already passed."

"That is terribly sad," Max said.

Chapter 4

Cleaning out the belongings of a loved one who has died is brutal. Max knew it all too well. She waited a few months after losing Adam and then, with the help of Char and Sawyer, her only child, completed the task as quickly as possible. The clothes were the easiest. Donate. But then she'd find a special shirt or jacket, and memories would flood in, distracting her from the task.

"I can still smell his cologne," she'd say, hugging the shirt and burying her face, delighting in the lingering scent of him. Sand sprinkled from the pockets of his swim trunks, left over from a day at the beach, and as it fell into the bedroom rug, Max worried about hearing it in the vacuum, certain the sound would catch her unprepared and spark memories of beach days and temporarily paralyze her.

"Will this ever get easier?" she lamented, then felt guilty for asking.

"Only with time," Char comforted. When Char lost her parents, Max had witnessed the toll it took. Sawyer chose to mask his feelings, staying stoic for his mother. This was his way. He was so like his father. Max watched him toss items into an oversized box. He stuffed it full, then packed it down and threw in a few more pieces.

"Where's the duct tape?" he asked. Max paused and watched him tightly secure the flaps of the box. She wanted to grab the tape and pull it off, to peek inside and check if there was anything she'd regret donating. She resisted.

"Goodwill?" she asked her son. "You can stack it with the others downstairs." Sawyer shot her a quizzical look.

"No, Mom. I'm keeping all of this." Relieved, Max opened her arms and when Sawyer came close, she enveloped him in a tight hug. There was so much to say, but no words.

"Mom, I understand if you decide to move from this house. I know it's soon, but it's okay. Dad would want us to be happy, not mired in our sadness. You know he'd hate that. It was hard for me to go back to school when I did, but ..." he trailed off.

"He always knew what was best."

"That's because he was the best," Char interrupted and joined them in the hug, reaching her arms around both of them.

"Alright. Back to it," Max said and hefted a thick pile of papers.

"Paperwork, shred."

Papers were easier to toss than clothing, but the

personal cards and notes and photos and little mementos of a person's life, what did one do with all of that? Trashing it seemed disrespectful, saving it too painful. After a full day, the three had narrowed the memorabilia down to a medium-sized box and had taken pictures of all the notes and cards and photos, creating a digital album.

So, when Max heard herself offering Larry Trawl help with sorting his deceased wife's belongings, she knew she must follow through even though she realized when he'd asked for help, he really meant he would not be involved and would hand her his house key and some boxes. *What was I thinking?*

"I'm sorry I dragged you into this," she said to Pearla as they hopped into Max's car.

"Don't worry about it. We're a team. With the two of us, it shouldn't take long, a couple hours at most. We can grab lunch after."

The drive to Larry Trawl's house was quick, only ten minutes. According to the locals, getting anywhere in the village was always quoted as ten minutes. Whether you were walking, biking, running, or driving—everything was ten minutes away. Max had laughed at this initially, but then as she settled into life in Silvermist Point, she realized the truth in it. Everything was, in fact, ten minutes away from everything else.

Larry and Colby had moved back to this home after Larry's estranged wife, Beth, died unexpectedly. She and Larry were separated at the time, in a stalemate regarding the housing situation of Colby. Beth refused to let Colby, in his fifties, and of questionable morals and character, live with them. Larry felt he had to keep a close watch over Colby, so the two had been sharing a broken-down trailer on the property of the inn. Sadly, Larry never reconciled with Beth before her untimely death.

Larry's grief was palpable; his face wore a perpetually pained expression. He still performed his duties as caretaker at the inn, but shared with Max his regret and how he missed Beth. Even Colby was sad, if not for Beth's death, at least for his father's loss. He finally agreed to seek treatment for his alcohol addiction and had earned his six-month sobriety chip, which he proudly showed off.

As they pulled into the driveway of the Trawls, Max took a deep breath, steeling herself for the task. They unloaded a stack of flattened boxes from the trunk. Pearla turned the key, and they stepped into the entryway. Thick beige carpet framed a small square of parquet wood flooring. A floral sofa and matching loveseat surrounded a coffee table draped in a doily with a vase of fake fabric flowers sitting on top. The room was sullen and dark with the heavy, embroidered draperies pulled closed.

"Should we remove our shoes?" Pearla whispered.

"Why are you whispering?" Max asked.

"I'm trying to be respectful. It's like a tomb in here." She strode across the room and flung open the curtains, letting the sunlight stream in.

"That's better."

The house was in decent shape, much less cluttered than Max expected. So many feminine touches. And clean. But that was because Larry had hired Emma, one of the inn's part-time housekeepers, to come twice a month. Max had never been inside before. *This is not what I imagined.*

The Celebration of Life for Beth Trawl was held on the grounds of the Snowy Plover Inn, and since then what had begun as a rocky and strained relationship between

Max, Pearla, and Larry Trawl, had shifted to something resembling a blossoming friendship. Colby still had a

ways to go. Baby steps.

They tried doors, first peeking into a small, tidy den. The next door revealed what must be Colby's room with its single, rumpled bed, posters of scantily clad models posing suggestively by monster trucks, empty soda cans, and heaps of laundry overflowing a hamper.

"Looks about right," Max said and rolled her eyes at Pearla.

"Wonder why he's still single?" Pearla quipped. They continued down the hallway and tried the next door. It was the master bedroom.

"It's so …" Pearla trailed off, as she scanned the room to take it all in. The bed had a thick mauve comforter with heavy fringe and was covered in about fifteen pillows of various sizes. The adjoining bathroom was pink from top to bottom. A shaggy carpet surrounded the toilet, and another hugged the lid. A crocheted cozy hid the extra roll of toilet paper. The women stared wide-eyed at one another, eyebrows raised, each daring the other not to burst out laughing, picturing Larry in his overalls and work boots in this dainty room and bathroom.

"Yikes! So much pink," Max finally said.

"Poor Larry," Pearla said, while examining a bottle of herbal bubble bath. The sunken tub was surrounded with specialty soaps and scented candles.

"I just can't see him indulging in a leisurely candlelit soak."

"Definitely not," Max agreed.

Wanting a plan and needing a place to begin, Max suggested starting with the closet. Larry had told her the large closet held most of Beth's clothes. Max slid the mirrored door open and was pleasantly surprised to observe that the walk-in was well organized. Shoes all lined up, sweaters in stacked shelves and blouses, jackets, dresses and pants hung according to season and color palette.

"I didn't know Beth well, but from what I remember, she was the jeans and sweatshirt type. No frills. I'm honestly surprised to see such a variety of clothing here. Some of these might fetch a decent price at Everything, Everything."

"Let's box those together."

Pearla climbed the step-ladder and pulled down a plastic storage tote from the highest shelf. She lifted the lid. It was stuffed with wigs.

"Wigs!" she exclaimed as she pulled a tight-curled blond wig over her own unruly chestnut hair.

"These are fabulous!" Pearla stepped out and preened in front of the full-length mirror.

"Don't get distracted. We have a job to do," Max said, but couldn't hide her smile. She wondered why Beth had such an extensive collection of wigs. Maybe she'd had chemotherapy at some point. That would explain it. She couldn't ask Larry. Too personal. As she and Pearla had gotten to know him, they'd realized he struggled with reading and writing and was functionally illiterate. Once they knew, they were mindful to give verbal directions and not leave notes as they had been doing. Colby, though he technically was literate, couldn't be relied upon as a messenger.

Larry Trawl was not an unintelligent man; he was profoundly gifted at fixing things others would have tossed. He had a keen eye for beauty and maintained the grounds of Snow Plover Inn such that they blended with, and stood apart from, the natural land. These skills were innate and Max appreciated him. The previous owners had requested Max allow Larry to keep his job, though he had saved for many years and didn't need the money.

"It's as much a part of him as breathing," Mable Evans had said. Max understood and planned to let Larry stay on as long as he wanted.

Pearla set up a portable speaker with country music tunes, and they worked in the closet for the next hour, removing clothes from hangers and sorting them into boxes. Larry's request was that everything be given to a women's shelter in Brookhaven. The only items he said not to donate were any pieces of jewelry. He didn't know what they might find, or what it was worth. Max had offered to have it appraised at E.E. Emporium.

"As long as you trust them to do right by Beth, that's fine with me," Larry agreed. "Whatever money the jewelry brings, I'll give it to the church. Beth would have wanted that. And if there's anything you want to keep, it's yours." It didn't escape Max and Pearla that he trusted them completely. Their relationship with the old caretaker had indeed come a long way since Max had purchased the inn and taken over when the former owners retired after over fifty years.

"Let's take a break. Larry said there are drinks in the fridge and we should help ourselves," Max said.

The kitchen was clean, like the rest of the house, excluding Colby's room. Inside the fridge they found juice, sodas, and cold bottled water. On the counter was a pink box from The Front Porch Bakery with "For You" scrawled on the top. It held six empanadas. They each took two and went to the back porch to eat them. Pearla found a lawn chair and plopped onto it.

"This one's chicken," Pearla said. "Yum!"

"Mine's spinach," Max said.

Max set down her soda and wandered around, holding an empanada in a napkin. An overgrown garden, in need of some weeding and care, was to the left. There was an orange tree, a lime, and what might be a peach tree. Behind the trees and toward the back of the yard were two stacks of hay bales set up with red painted bulls-eye targets. Behind the hay bales, she saw piles of soda cans with dents and holes in them and some covered in paint. *I don't want to know. This is not my business. I shouldn't be snooping.*

Pearla called from the porch. "Max, you've got to see this. Look what I found." As Max jogged over, she had a sinking feeling. Pearla's tone sounded concerned. Pearla stood next to an open storage box on the patio and was aiming her phone at the contents inside.

"I was looking for a cushion," she said. Max leaned in. Lying on the patio chair cushions were two guns, a slingshot, and a bow.

"What the hell? Isn't Colby still technically on parole?"

"Maybe these are Larry's ... or Beth's?" Pearla said hopefully while snapping pictures. "We should report this to Rene."

It was fair to say that both ladies knew Sheriff Rene Silva would either make a huge deal of the situation and blow it all out of proportion, or equally possible, make light of it and brush it off. Neither reaction seemed optimal.

"Should we tell him, though? I vote no. I don't want Larry getting in trouble. He's been through enough," Max said. "And he's finally trusting us; we don't want to jeopardize that."

"I agree. We saw nothing," Pearla said.

Max pointed to the far end of the yard. "There are targets set up at the back of the property, just behind those fruit trees. These are probably just pellet guns or maybe paintball guns."

"Yeah, we're overreacting. Colby wouldn't be stupid enough to have real guns here, and he's been working so hard to stay on the straight and narrow," Pearla said with little conviction as she replaced the lid on the storage box and snapped it shut.

"We saw nothing," Max said. "Let's go finish the job. We never came out here."

"Nope, never," Pearla muttered as they made their way back to the closet.

She pulled the final two boxes down from the top shelf and blew off some dust before popping the lid of a plastic file box. Nestled inside were two shoe boxes, sneakers, women's size nine. Both had SMPOV written in black marker on the lids. Her eyes grew wide, and she sucked in a breath.

"Do you think these are…?"

"*Silvermist Point of View*?" Max finished the thought.

"Jackpot!" Pearla yelled when she peered inside.

As they pulled out the tri-folded copies of the newsletters in various pastel shades, Max wondered how far back they went. The oldest she found was from twenty-five years ago.

"It doesn't prove Beth was the author. Even though it stopped with her death," Max said.

"And she saved every copy? I think we've solved that mystery," Pearla responded, then added, "These are a really cool archive of the village. We can't just toss them."

"Definitely not. These belong in a book. It's like the town's history."

"As told in gossip."

"We can ask Andrew or Tom if they might know how to publish it. I'm sure they'd be interested in carrying copies at Books and Brew."

"Great idea."

"But not until we've read them all first."

"What's in the last box?" Pearla opened it and began pulling out scraps of paper with handwritten notes, receipts, and photos.

"Let's take it with us," Max said. "We can go through it later when we have more time."

Max and Pearla stacked the boxes to be donated and left them for Larry to take in his truck. They took with them the box of newsletters, the box of scraps, and the few pieces of jewelry they'd found in Beth's dresser drawer, along with a wooden jewelry box. They loaded it all into the trunk of the car and intended to go through it later. For today, they were done with the job and eager to get back to the inn.

Chapter 5

Pearla

Pearla found Emma folding a load of pool towels from the dryer in the laundry room. She was glad they hired her. Emma was a pleasant girl and an efficient worker.

"I'll be back tomorrow to clean the rooms listed on the schedule and tidy the pool area. I can do the common rooms too."

"That's perfect, Emma. I hope you know how much we appreciate you."

"I do. Thank you," Emma said on her way out.

Pearla proceeded to walk through the grounds. She passed the pool where a couple of teenage boys lounged in the sun. Pearla smiled, noticing one was reading a book. Poor cell reception had its advantages. At Royal High, where she'd worked with Max, it was rare to see teens without earbuds in place or walking, head down, and oblivious to their surroundings. She came around the side, passing the fire pit, and intending to enter the inn through the front. A guest stood near the steps, fidgeting, swiping his forearm across his brow, and checking his watch. He was middle-aged with what Pearla thought of as a dad bod, sporting gray nylon golf pants that were a shade too tight.

"Hi, Mr. Taylor. Is there anything I can help you with?" Pearla asked, as she noticed the perplexed expression on his face.

"Well, I figured I could get an Uber to take me to the golf course property. I'm supposed to meet with the sellers today, but didn't think it through. Had no idea it would be this challenging. I don't have my car with me. Tried calling Pete Worley, but he's not picking up and I don't have the other brothers' numbers. I'm afraid they'll think I'm a no-show."

Wanting to put him at ease, Pearla gave him a comforting smile. "I'm happy to give you a ride. It's not far. Would you mind if Max, the owner, tagged along as well? To be honest, we've been wanting to see the property ourselves, but haven't had the chance to get over there." Pearla thought for a second, then quickly added, "Don't worry, we're not planning to buy it." Relief flooded the man's face.

"I'd be truly grateful for the ride. Could we leave right now? I don't want to show up late."

"Let me grab my keys. Give me two minutes," Pearla said. She ran over to Max's cottage, hoping to find her there and grab her spare set of car keys. The door was unlocked, and Max was in her kitchen adding foam to a freshly poured cappuccino.

"Max, you'll have to drink it later. We're driving Bruce Taylor to the Worley Property." Max set her coffee down and followed Pearla, slipping on her shoes near the front door.

"Don't you dare lick the foam, Butters," she admonished her portly cat as she went out the door.

"You know he will," Pearla laughed. "He's heading there now."

After thanking the ladies profusely, Bruce Taylor asked them what they thought of the town and whether they believed the property should be developed.

"We only recently learned it was once a golf property," Max said.

"As for the town," Pearla added, "it's perfect. At least in my opinion."

"Hmm," Bruce answered. It wasn't clear if he was agreeing or not. "Could you please turn up the air conditioning?"

"Sure," Pearla obliged. She wanted to ask more questions about his intentions for the land should he acquire it, but before she got the chance, they pulled up to the property where two men in golf attire stood at the opening of the chain-link fencing. *They must be the Worley brothers.* The taller one was pointedly checking his watch. Bruce jumped out of the car as soon as Pearla stopped and hustled over.

"Sorry for the delay, I should have known it would be tough to get an Uber here," he said, slightly out of breath. "These ladies graciously gave me a lift."

"Well, you're here now, so let's walk the property and we'll answer any questions best we can. I'm Pete Worley.

And this is my brother, Evan. Seth, our other brother, should be here shortly."

"We'll see if he shows up," Evan said under his breath with a hint of sarcasm.

Seth must be the one who's not wanting to sell. Pearla figured they were skipping introductions of her and Max, so she interjected, offering a handshake.

"Hi, I'm Pearla, the general manager of the Snowy Plover Inn. We spoke on the phone. And this is Maxine, the owner. If you don't mind, we'd love to see the property as well."

Evan eyed her up and down, while shaking her hand, then Max's. Pete said, "Sure. Why not?" and didn't offer his hand.

The family resemblance was clear. Pete was the slightly taller of the two and had a medium build with a slight paunch accentuated by a too-tight nylon golf shirt. His face was ruddy and puffy, and his well-groomed hair was more gray than brown. *Looks like he enjoys the booze.*

Evan was better looking, with an athletic build and tanned skin. Both had an arrogant air about them, walking side by side with long strides and puffed out chests.

"Here's where we've cleared out the area," Evan pointed. "Are you a lefty or a righty, Bruce? We've got loaner clubs for both so you can get a feel for the course. You're a golfer, right?"

"I dabble a little. I'm not real good at it, but I play occasionally, just for fun." He picked up a driver and swung it a few times, spreading his feet apart and practicing his stance.

"This first hole is a par four." Max and Pearla stood back and watched as the three men teed off. Then they followed them as they walked to where the balls landed.

"That must be the old clubhouse," Max murmured to Pearla as she pointed to a structure that was gutted and burned. "I can definitely see the potential here. This is impressive, and it's a hundred and fifty acres total. A golf course makes the most sense. I'd hate to see housing go in. A golf course would still keep it kinda wild, and open."

"How awful to remove any of these beautiful trees," Pearla said, admiring the pines, oaks and others she wasn't sure of. The men were now putting to the hole as best Pearla could figure. Neither she nor Max understood the game. *As long as we keep out of the way.*

On the next hole, Bruce overshot and was practice-swinging how best to extricate his ball from the wilds and back onto the green. Out of the corner of her eye, Pearla saw it happen. Bruce Taylor took aim, swung back his club and before he could swing forward to drive his ball, a flying object coming from out of the woods hit him square in the middle of the forehead. He fell to the ground, flat on his back.

Stunned, no one moved, as each person present was replaying and questioning whether they had really witnessed what just occurred. After a brief pause, the Worley brothers, Max, and Pearla ran over. A distinct dent about the size and impression of a golf ball was rapidly reddening in the middle of Bruce Taylor's forehead, and trickles of blood dripped out of both ears.

"What the hell just happened?" Evan asked.

"Where did that come from?" Pete frantically spun around, scanning the wooded area behind them.

"Is someone gonna check him out?" Pearla asked as she bent down and gently shook Bruce's shoulders.

"Max, call an ambulance. This is bad. He's not breathing." Pearla wracked her brain to remember how to give chest compressions and began as best she could.

"Probably just lost consciousness," Evan said way too casually.

How can he be so flippant?

"No, this is serious," Max said as she dialed 911 and reported the accident. She switched the phone to speaker mode when the operator asked if anyone was giving him CPR.

"Yes," Max explained, then she and Pearla took turns, while the men stood staring at them.

"We may need you to tag in," Max said, already feeling her arms tiring.

"Sorry. Sorry, yes, let me take over." Evan got on his knees and awkwardly took over.

"Help is on the way; the ambulance should be there in less than five minutes," the operator said. When the ambulance arrived, the two technicians hovered over Bruce Taylor and tried to revive him. The small group stood in shocked silence as the emergency medical technician officially pronounced him dead.

"Dead?" Pearla asked. "As in dead, dead?" *Is there any other kind of dead?*

"Yes, unfortunately. I'm sorry, ma'am. Is, I mean, was he your husband?" the EMT asked.

"No. He was a guest at our inn," Max said.

"Ah, yes, the Snowy Plover, right?"

Pearla and Max both nodded. There wasn't much else to say. Sheriff Silva pulled up minutes behind the ambulance and offered a quick hello to Max and Pearla before visually surveying the scene and asking, "Someone want to tell me what happened here?"

"Accident, sir," Evan said. "Terrible accident."

When Evan elaborated no further, Sheriff Silva turned to Pearla and raised his eyebrows. She understood he was asking her to fill in the blanks.

"It was all so fast. I mean, one minute, Mr. Taylor, Bruce, was swinging his club, aiming to get his ball back to the hole. I don't really know the game all that well, and the next thing I saw, he was hit by something. I assume it was a golf ball straight between the eyes." *That probably wasn't too helpful.*

"Okay, who hit the ball that struck Mr. Taylor? Where did it come from?" Rene Silva asked impatiently. Pete Worley was wringing his hands nervously while shifting his weight from foot to foot.

"It came from the woods. That direction." Pete pointed. The others nodded in agreement.

"Who shot it?" Rene asked again. No one answered. "Well, didn't anyone yell out that a man was hit?"

"I did," Pete said defensively. "No one came forward."

The incident had occurred so quickly and was so shocking and unexpected. It had to be someone messing around, trespassing on the property. A gruesome, tragic accident. Still, no one would likely come forward to admit they were there illegally, and that they knocked someone in the head.

"I think we were all just so stunned," Max said. "None of us thought to investigate who hit the ball."

"That's exactly right," Pete agreed. Then he surprised Pearla by asking, "Sheriff, do you think someone did this on purpose?"

Funny, he would jump to that conclusion.

"I mean, there are people who don't want my family to sell. We've received some strongly worded letters."

"That's too far-fetched," Evan interjected. "I can't believe anyone has that good of aim and timing, to take out a man. It's not like he was shot with a gun. It was only a golf ball."

"We are assuming it was a golf ball," Pearla corrected. "It happened so fast. We don't know for certain."

"Well, I don't like it. Any time a person gets killed, accident or otherwise, I need an explanation. I'll have to investigate this. Are there any other people who have access to the property?" Rene Silva pulled his familiar yellow notepad from his pocket and flipped a couple of pages, then began to write.

Pete spoke up, "Sheriff, it's common knowledge that folks use this property all the time—despite the keep-out signs—for hiking, illegal camping, trails to the beach, paintballing, and apparently golfing in the wilds. It could have been anyone, and I'm sure they're long gone after hearing the sirens."

"My guess is, it was a kid messing around. They're always trespassing," Evan said.

"In fact, that's one of the many reasons we're selling it," Pete explained. "People are constantly trespassing, no one heeds the signs, and if someone gets hurt, I have no doubt they'll try to pin it on us somehow and sue. It's bullshit." Pete covered his mouth as if he'd said too much.

"Well, now I suppose we only have three interested buyers. Less competition." Was this Evan's attempt to lighten the mood?

The comment fell flat. Rene Silva cleared his throat. "All right, let's start with this. Where's the golf ball that struck the deceased? I'll need to take it."

No one spoke up. Directed by Sheriff Silva, they searched the area for the offending golf ball turned weapon. None was located.

"It should be right around here," Rene said in a voice tinged with irritation. "Did one of you move it?"

No one responded verbally, only shrugged in disbelief at the question. Now that the body had been carted away, the surrounding area looked untouched as normal, other than extra sets of footprints and tire tracks, but certainly not as though someone lost their life here.

Pearla jumped in, unable to resist commenting and saying her private thoughts out loud: "There were two EMTs and there are five of us. Let's look at how many different sets of footprints we see." She looked at Rene for approval. "Wouldn't that be a place to start? The ground is soft here, off the grass. There should be only eight prints in total. If there's a ninth type, then someone removed the ball while we were distracted."

"Oh, Pearla. You're quite the sleuth. If only it were that simple. There's no way to identify eight distinct shoe prints in this damp ground."

"Thanks for the compliment," Pearla said. "I'm curious, Sheriff, what is your plan?"

Sheriff Silva walked into the woods and called over his shoulder. "I'm gonna have a look around. See if anything strikes me as out of place. Did you notice any cars parked outside the fence when you got here?"

No one had.

"Sheriff, if there's nothing else you need from us, we're heading out," Evan said.

"I'll be in touch. I'll need formal statements from both

of you," Rene called.

It took Pearla less than a minute to decide to follow Sheriff Silva into the woods. Her curiosity had the best of her, and one look at Max confirmed that she, too, was willing to follow. Just past the area that had been cleared for the course, the property was wild and filled with bushes and trees and the ground was covered in leaves and pine needles and soft, damp dirt. However, it was obvious that it was not untouched by humans, regardless of fencing and keep-out signage. Pearla admitted to herself: Rene was right. There was no way to distinguish individual shoe prints. They continued farther in.

"What's this?" Pearla asked and held up a small yellow cylinder.

"That's a Nerf blaster bullet," Max said. "Sawyer and his friends were obsessed with them when he was little."

Rene pointed to a clump of trees and bushes. "See the paint splotches? Those are from paintballers. It's a popular sport. And this right here?" He indicated a long swipe in the soft ground. "This could be where someone shot a golf ball, but it's too far from where Bruce Taylor was hit."

"Right," Max agreed.

They picked their way through the property, unsure of what they were looking for. Though they managed to recover six golf balls, it only served to prove that this was something trespassers used the property for, which was widely known already.

"Let's consider the access points to the property. That could help us figure out where whoever hit the ball got in," Pearla suggested.

"There are quite a few breaches in the fencing. Plus, there's access from the cliffside leading to the beach," Rene said, as they walked on.

The exploration of the property led to no further speculation or information that could explain what happened. Pearla thought there would be no reason for someone to come forward, especially if it was a kid who shot the ball, for fear of getting in trouble. *It seemed so deliberate. How could it be an accident?*

"Probably an unfortunate accident," Sheriff Silva commented, as if reading her mind. "I'll go ahead and write up a report, and I'll inform the family. I may need to confirm his address with you. That'll be the quickest way to look up next-of-kin."

"Sure," Max said. "Whatever we can do to assist."

They said goodbye and parted ways. Max and Pearla walked in silence to the car and got in. They turned to each other at the same time and Pearla spoke first.

"So, I don't actually believe it was an accident, do you?"

"Definitely not. What are the chances someone randomly just happened to hit a ball that happened to strike this guy right between the eyes? Zero percent chance."

"Yes, but even if it was planned, how could anyone have that kind of precision?" Both women sat silently to ponder that. It made no sense.

"We shouldn't get involved," Max concluded.

"Let's just mind our own business." Pearla nodded, knowing it would be best to keep out of it. Max's phone rang, breaking the silence. She glanced at the screen.

"It's Char."

"Oh, answer it. Put her on speaker."

Char's voice filled the car. "Max, hey. I'm glad I caught you."

"Char, you're on speaker. Pearla and I are driving back

from the golf property. We just checked it out, and you won't believe what happened."

"That's the acreage you told me about, right? I've been thinking about it a lot. Maybe I should try to buy it. I could build my dream house there. It's not been sold yet, has it?"

An ear-to-ear grin broke across Max's face as Pearla let out a whoop.

"That would be amazing. How soon can you get here? You'd want to see it in person, right?" Max asked.

"It has to be soon," Pearla added enthusiastically. "There are other potential buyers, all scheduled to tour it this week. We think they may want to develop it, but Char, you might have a shot. We overheard one of the Worley brothers say he's against development. But I suppose it would depend on what you'd be willing to pay."

"Ugh," Char groaned. "I can't come until at least next week. There's no way. I'm on a safari, remember? I'll need you two to decide if it's a good choice for me."

Max smiled at Pearla.

"In our totally unbiased opinion, we think you should put in an offer," Pearla said. "We can get a sense of what the others are willing to pay and let you know. There are only three others."

"I thought there were four investors interested. Are there only three now? Did one drop out?"

"Technically, yes. He dropped out because he dropped dead." Max went on to give Char the short version of what had just taken place. Char agreed it was highly suspicious and asked them to keep her up to date.

"I'll message you tomorrow. I better get some sleep since I'm expected to get up in only four hours," Char said.

"Keep those photos coming, and we'll talk soon,"

Pearla said.

Then, to Max after she hung up, "That would be so great if Char bought the property. Let's see if we can make it happen."

Chapter 6

Monday
Maxine

When Max arrived at The Front Porch Bakery, her heart temporarily stopped when she saw a basket of lavender pastel, tri-folded newsletters sitting next to the entrance. It couldn't be. She picked one up and stared at the title, "*Silvermist Point of View.*" She grabbed the basket, and held it up, asking the barista, "Where did you get these?" as she stood in the doorway.

"They were on the porch, right there, when I arrived this morning. The customers are really excited about them. I haven't had a chance to look at one yet. Apparently, this newsletter is really popular. I'd never heard of it before today."

"I have. It's town gossip. I'd hardly call it news," Max said disdainfully as she put the basket down and plopped into an Adirondack chair on the porch.

Tee Time Tragedy! (The headline shouted off the page)

Yesterday as the Worley brothers showed the golf course property, a lush area of approximately 150 acres on the outskirts of Silvermist Point, to a prospective buyer, the buyer was struck by an unidentified flying object, presumably a golf ball, and DIED at the scene. Rumors of the property being cursed, have resurfaced.

It should be noted that the deceased was staying at the Snowy Plover Inn, the very same inn where just months ago an attempted murder occurred and a dead body washed up on the shoreline. Coincidence???

Really, with the triple question marks? The rest of the newsletter was filled with non-offensive tidbits, a word search and a promise that the SMPOV was back in business, and readers could expect unbiased news of the town biweekly. Unbiased, my ass. Max wanted to take all remaining copies with her, but she knew the attempt to conceal the story would be futile if, as before, copies of the newsletter were all over town. She grabbed her order and rushed back to the inn.

"Good thing you went for the fresh baguettes," Pearla said. "Or when would we have seen this? The inn obviously is not included on the list of delivery points."

"Who is responsible? I thought Beth was the one who wrote these. Did someone else take over?" Max asked.

"Sure looks that way."

Chapter 7

Pearla

Against their initial instinct, Max and Pearla thought it best to do some investigating of their own. If someone wanted Bruce Taylor dead, it stood to reason it would be one of the other three investors, trying to limit his competition. They strategized how to broach the subject and decided to imply that Sheriff Silva was going to question the hotel guests about their whereabouts and by the way, where were you yesterday while Bruce Taylor was touring the property?

Max found a way to bring it up with J.T. Fields by first showing him the SMPOV newsletter and gauging his reaction. She reported to Pearla that he had expressed surprise and concern, but she couldn't decide if he was being genuine or not. Next, she explained that the sheriff wanted to account for the inn's guests' whereabouts yesterday, so where was he? J.T. explained he was walking the beach during the timeframe in question. When Max asked if anyone was with him, he said no. Did he see anyone else at the beach or on his walk down? Also no. Then he changed his mind and said he saw two teenage boys. Max thanked him for his cooperation, then asked when he was scheduled to tour the property.

"I asked him, as if I was entitled to know, and he told me he's meeting with the owners this afternoon," she reported to Pearla.

"What is your gut feeling about him?" Pearla asked.

"He's intimidating, and he knows it. He's so tall, I felt like he was towering over me. As to whether he's telling the truth, I'm not certain he is," Max said.

* * *

Pearla had used a similar tactic with Jason Martinez, stopping him as he passed through the reception area carrying a daypack.

"Headed out, Mr. Martinez?" He turned and strode over, smiling. Tall and fit, he was a handsome man, though not Pearla's type and too old for her, she mused.

"Yes, I thought I'd take a drive around, you know, explore a bit. I might borrow a bike later on."

"That's lovely. It's a beautiful day," Pearla said, then got right to it. "Where were you yesterday afternoon? I'm sure you heard about the accident." He raised his eyebrows.

"Yes, tragic." After a pause, he put on his sunglasses and turned to walk away.

"Wait. I was wondering where you were when it happened?"

"Not sure why you're asking, but I was in Brookhaven. Now if that's all, I'll be on my way." Pearla would not let him go so easily. "I'm asking because I know the sheriff will. Where did you go in Brookhaven?" Pearla knew she was pushing her luck and had no business asking, but she was in this deep, so why not?

"I got lunch at a burger joint." Pearla heard the annoyance in his voice.

"Was it Brookhaven Burgers? I love that place."

"Yes, that was it. I'm leaving now and the sheriff can ask me himself if he needs any other information. Have a good day." He turned his back and left the building.

She recounted the interaction for Max, who concluded, "Weak alibi. Sounds like he is purposely being vague."

Pearla got an idea. "I've got time to go to Brookhaven Burgers, I can check out his story. I'll show them our copy of his driver's license and see if they recognize him. My gut tells me he's hiding something. It may have nothing to do with Bruce Taylor's death, but he's sketchy."

"Can't hurt to look into it," Max said. "Text or call if you learn anything."

"Will do."

Pearla stopped at the office and grabbed the photocopy she'd taken of Jason Martinez's driver's license. It was grainy when she enlarged it, but it would have to do. As she drove with her window down, salt air caressed her face as the scent of the pine woods on either side of the narrow highway wafted in. *I'm so blessed to call this place home.* It wasn't long before she saw the sign welcoming visitors to Brookhaven. Pearla was familiar with the town and after locating the burger joint, pulled her car into its small parking lot.

Not sure how best to approach the staff about the photo, she took a seat and ordered her favorite menu item, a bleu cheese burger, well done, with pickles, grilled onions, and ketchup, and a large cream soda. When the friendly waiter brought her food, she asked him if he had worked yesterday afternoon. When he said yes, she unfolded the photo and showed it to him.

"Did you happen to serve this man yesterday? Or do you recognize him?" The waiter looked at her quizzically and Pearla thought fast. "He's an old college friend of my father. I told Dad I'd try to locate him. My father's not well…" Pearla paused and sniffed, marveling at how seamlessly the lie slid out. She looked expectantly at the server.

"My goodness. I'm sorry. I can't help you though. I didn't see him yesterday. We weren't busy, so I'm positive I'd remember." Pearla sighed.

"That's okay. It was a longshot, but I thought I'd check." She took a bite of the burger. "Magnificent! But I know I won't finish it. Can I get the check and a to-go box when you get a chance?"

Pearla enjoyed a few more bites before packing up the rest in the provided container. Once she was settled in her car, she called Max.

"Well, that was a bust, but at least I got one of their burgers. I'm heading back now."

"Hey, would you mind picking up some cat kibble for Butters? He's being picky and won't eat the one I got from Miscellaneous Goods. I'll text you a picture of the one he likes." Pearla smiled.

"Anything for Butty. We can't have him skipping meals." They both laughed picturing Butters who could definitely survive a skipped meal or two. Max liked to joke that he was "big boned."

"Wait, before you hang up, I saw something interesting. It was right after you left for Brookhaven."

In her excitement, Pearla gripped the steering wheel. "Tell me."

"Mr. Martinez and Mr. Fields were talking in the courtyard, and it looked intense, raised voices and lots of gesticulating. I couldn't make out the specifics, though. Just as Martinez walked off, I came out and asked Fields if everything was okay. He was like, 'Fine, fine. Everything's fine. I'm sure you know we're after the same thing.' And I said, 'Yes, the Worley property.' Then he nodded and walked away."

"Hmmm. That's interesting. Has Nolan Briggs checked in yet?"

"No, he called earlier. Said he'll be checking in late. Also said he had an appointment at the property, but he doesn't think he'll make it on time."

"That means the other two will go without him. I wonder if that gives him an advantage."

"Only if he knows what the other offers are," Max said.

"What time is the meeting? We should be there. We can try to get an idea of what the investors are willing to pay."

"I'll see if I can find out. I'm going on a bike ride first to get rid of some nervous energy."

Chapter 8

Maxine

Max thought a bike ride might help her clear her mind. It was such a gorgeous day, no fog in sight, just a bright blue sky and crisp air. *I'm glad I had Larry restore these beach cruisers; it's a nice little extra to offer our guests.* There were four bikes in all, the two white ones were women's style, and the two aqua ones were men's, though it didn't really matter. Max preferred the women's style so she could jump down easily to stop without tipping over. One of the aqua bikes was gone, as well as one of the white ones. Max rolled out the other white bike and grabbed a helmet from the rack, in case she wanted to ride out to the main road. Better safe than sorry.

She rode around the circular driveway a few times to

get her bearings before deciding to head to the village.

"Hey, Max. Are you just starting out? Nice day for a ride." It was Misty Caldwell, one of their current long-term guests, looking perfect, pedaling in her white capris, a powder blue boat neck shirt and sandals, no helmet to mess up her hair.

"Hey, Misty. I wish I'd known you were riding. I'd have gone with you. I haven't been on a bike in a while and today looks like the perfect day for a ride."

Max liked Misty Caldwell, though her first impression had not been positive. She'd never trusted women who had a lot of cosmetic procedures; fair or not, it was how she felt. Misty was one of those women. Her upturned, button nose was too perfect with its shiny diamond stud. She had long, feathery eyelashes and eyes rimmed in what looked like permanent tattooed eyeliner, with high cheekbones, that must have been created with filler, and a dewy glow on flawless skin. Her comically plump lips were always a shade too bright, and her highlighted hair was styled to look like it wasn't, but Max knew better. Misty's makeup alone left Max feeling plain and underdressed, even though this was how she was most comfortable. *There is no one I need to impress.*

Max's style was casual and comfortable. She rarely accessorized, and she applied her neutral-shade makeup with a light touch. To Max, dressing up meant a long, gauzy skirt. She kept her nails short and if she painted them, it was a nude shade that disguised the chips. This was how she felt most at ease, but somehow being around another woman who expended such energy on her outward appearance made Max ponder if she should pay more attention to her own. She knew what her husband, Adam, would say, as she heard his voice in her mind. "Nonsense! You're a natural beauty, and you look great no matter how you're dressed." Then he'd take her in his arms.

Max did not think she'd like Misty, but she did. Misty was bubbly and fun, and an impressive businesswoman. Misty had reserved the two small upstairs guest rooms of the inn that shared a common bathroom down the hall, for the next eight months, possibly longer, and she'd paid the full amount up front. One for her and one for her construction foreman, Jack Caldwell, to use if he needed it.

"I want to make sure I have a comfortable place to stay. I can't live in a construction zone with the constant noise and dust. This way, I can be on site whenever I need to without driving two hours from my other house. And your inn is a dream."

Max and Pearla had gotten to know Misty since she practically lived at the inn, and they'd all become friends. Misty promised them free treatments at the spa when it opened, and rather than feeling in competition with her, Max and Pearla were excited about the wellness center and spa. If anything, it would lead more people to discover the village of Silvermist Point.

There wasn't much else around the wellness center property. Mirror Lake was undeveloped, and Brookhaven was nearly an hour away. Silvermist Point could be a nice distraction and the Snowy Plover Inn was a much lower price point than the suites and rooms would be at the Getaway Ranch. The Getaway might get the business of people who wanted to visit for just the day. Win, win.

Marjory Jones was excited about Getaway Ranch, too. She and Misty discussed the possibility of a second Gracious Grapes tasting room located on the property. In fact, Misty made a point to offer any of the retailers in Silvermist Point an opportunity to sell products in the shop on her property, saying she didn't want to take business away from the town; she was all about partnering for the good of all. Misty knew how to get folks to like her.

Townsfolk were much more reticent about the Worley property than the Getaway Ranch and Spa. It was right inside the town limits of Silvermist Point and its development would directly affect the town and its residents. Whether that would be a good or bad thing was yet to be determined in their minds. Most of the homes in Silvermist were older and stayed within families, passed down from one generation to the next. Many were vacation homes and not occupied full time, keeping the permanent resident population low. There wasn't any traffic and people trusted their neighbors.

Misty pulled her bike up next to Max and jumped off. "I saw one of the investors on the other bike," she said. "He was wearing golf clothes, so I asked him if he was going to tour the property and try out the course. He said he was."

"I was hoping to go as well," Max confided. "Char's considering buying it, but I wanted to get an idea of what the others would offer. I need an excuse to be there. I don't want to seem nosey."

Misty looked thoughtful. "You know, the Worleys were in touch with me before they put it on the market. They were trying to get me to purchase it as part of the Getaway. I can't though. I'm already way over my head and I don't need another project of that scope."

Max had an idea. "Misty, will you come with me to the Worley property? You can pretend you're reconsidering.

You can be my excuse for being there. I haven't told them about Char's interest, yet. Would you mind?"

"No, not at all. We should probably go now if we want to catch them. I'll drive us." Max rolled the bike back. She'd have to ride later. This was more important.

Chapter 9

Sheriff Rene Silva

Rene Silva made the call to Bruce Taylor's wife informing her of the tragic accident. He hated this part of his job. Death was never easy, and he couldn't help but get emotional when he thought of the loved ones of the deceased and how their lives would be forever changed after his phone call relaying the news.

One thing he enjoyed about Silvermist Point was the relative peacefulness. Most days he patrolled the small village in his cruiser, stopped in to visit various establishments, and wrote the occasional ticket for an expired registration or non-functional brake lights. It was light duty and low stress. He appreciated flexing his detective muscles now and then, though. Important to keep the brain sharp.

He eased the cruiser onto the two-lane highway just outside the village. He planned to do a quick patrol of the hill areas, go back to his office next to Janice at the Post Stop to shuffle some papers, patrol again to make his presence known, then cash it in for the day and relax with a drink while binge-watching a cop show on his sixty-inch TV, with Earl Gray curled and purring at his feet. It was not to be.

Rene noticed long black skid marks on the road and felt his pulse quicken. Those were not there before. Someone must have tried to avoid hitting an animal, probably a deer. Rene had a soft spot for wildlife. The skid marks veered off the highway to the side of the road where the gravel was stirred up. Hating to see an animal injured and in pain, he decided to go back and look in the ditch. He hoped he wouldn't have to put an injured animal out of its misery.

Executing a perfect U-turn, he pulled over and clicked on the flashers. The woods were thick on both sides of the highway and there was a steep ditch on the side where the skid marks stopped. It wasn't likely that an entire car had ended up in the ditch. It wasn't that deep. However, it was deep enough for a man and his mangled bicycle to be hidden from passersby, and that is exactly what the sheriff saw when he peered over the edge.

"Holy smokes!" he shouted to no one.

He called for an ambulance, then scrambled down the ledge to check on the man whose badly injured body lay at the bottom. A few feet away lay the bicycle with a plastic placard attached to the front: Property of the Snowy Plover Inn.

"Rene? Sheriff? Is that you? Are you okay? Is there anything I can help with? What happened here?"

Sheriff Silva instantly recognized Pearla's voice, firing

off questions as she approached from the road above. "It's a bike accident!" he shouted back. "Stay back. Don't come closer."

But then she was standing at the edge of the ditch. He looked up at her as she covered her mouth with both hands, eyes wide. "Oh, no! Is he dead?"

"I'm about to check his breathing and his pulse. I just got here. Recognize the bike?" he asked.

Pearla's words came in a rush. "Yes, that's one of ours, and that man is Jason Martinez. He's staying at the inn."

Rene was on his knees, examining the man.

"I don't feel a pulse, and he's not breathing." Rene knew he was dead. His skin was clammy, and he already felt a little stiff.

"How can this be?" Pearla started to cry. Rene moved up the embankment to stand next to her and put a comforting arm around her shoulders.

"I'm sorry you had to see this."

"I should leave," Pearla said.

"Yes, I think you should. Drive carefully," Rene responded, then immediately second-guessed himself, wondering if there was a way he could have offered Pearla more compassion. It was a shock to see a dead body and now she'd seen two in two days.

Never mind. Rene accepted he would not get home early. By the time he checked in with the main police office in Brookhaven and put out a statement, he'd be delayed by hours. He called Janice.

"Janice, can you put something out on the neighborhood app? There's been an accident on the highway. A man is dead. Ask for information and witnesses and provide the tip line number, please."

Rene knew the postmaster and purveyor of all things gossip would run with the information. It would travel through the nerves of the town with remarkable speed. Accuracy be damned. This was by far the fastest way to locate any potential witnesses. It wouldn't be the first time Janice had provided him with intel on the townspeople. And she usually knew how to be discreet.

The thing was, this man was not a local, but a visitor. And he was the second person interested in buying the Worley property to die unnaturally in the last two days. Was there someone who didn't want the property sold who would go to this length to orchestrate these deaths? Might they be taking out the competition one by one?

Chapter 10

Pearla

As Pearla walked back to her car, her stomach twisted, and she wiped away stubborn tears. To see a man in his prime left for dead was deeply disturbing, more so since it occurred in her own town. A wave of guilt washed over her anxiety. Jason Martinez, now dead in a literal ditch, had been her prime suspect in yesterday's demise of Bruce Taylor. Now, fifty percent of the prospective investors were out of the running to purchase the property.

Not ready to drive yet, she gulped some deep breaths, then called Max, hoping her phone was within reach and not silenced. Max picked up.

"Can you talk privately?" Pearla asked.

"Yes, just a sec." Pearla heard voices in the background

and Max's steps as she walked away.

"I'm at the property," Max said quietly. "We found out they were showing it and Misty drove us. Did you know the Worleys approached her to see if she wanted to buy it? We're here with J.T. Fields and all three of the Worley brothers. The youngest one, Seth, arrived late, but he's here now. It's interesting to watch the family dynamics. Oh, and Jason Martinez hasn't shown up yet. Only J.T. Fields is here, and I can't tell if he's a serious buyer or not."

Pearla interrupted, unable to wait one more second for Max to pause. "Max! Jason Martinez is dead." Somehow speaking the words aloud brought the tears again.

"What? When? Oh my God, *how*?"

Pearla explained what she had witnessed on her way back from Brookhaven.

"I have so many questions. Can you meet Misty and me at Barnaby's? I think we all could use a drink."

Pearla readily agreed. She drove as if she was on autopilot, ending up in the parking lot at Barnaby's not fully cognizant of how she got there. She spat on the napkin from Brookhaven Burgers and rubbed at the mascara smudges under her eyes, then applied a bit of face powder before going in.

"Iced tea?" Kelly called from behind the bar as soon as Pearla entered through the back door.

"No. Kelly, I need alcohol today. An 805, please. No glass." Pearla trudged in and slid onto one of the bar stools, sighing. Kelly passed her the frosty bottle. She took large swigs, draining half the beer before she set it down. She folded her hands together to quell the shakiness and took a few calming breaths.

Kelly looked at her with concerned eyes. "You okay?"

"Just shaken up. There was an accident on the highway.

A man is dead."

"You saw it? Tyne got an alert on his phone a few minutes ago from the neighborhood app asking for witnesses."

"No, it'd already happened, but I pulled over when I noticed Sheriff Silva's patrol car. I wish I hadn't; I wasn't mentally prepared to see that." Her body gave an involuntary shudder.

"Was it a hit and run? What type of horrible human would do such a thing?" Kelly said as Tyne joined her behind the bar.

"That's what I was thinking. Whoever it is, I hope they're caught and made to pay." Tyne's eyes flashed with anger.

"It's hard to say what happened. I think that's why the sheriff is asking for witnesses," Pearla explained. It was suspicious though.

When Max and Misty arrived, they moved to a booth.

Pearla was on her second beer and feeling lightheaded. "I should eat something." Then she remembered the barely touched leftover burger, and hoped it wouldn't spoil in the car.

Max said to just go get it. They were ordering food anyway, and Tyne wouldn't care if she brought the burger in and ate it. She hurried out to get it and spotted Jack Morehouse, Misty's construction foreman, in the lot.

"Hi, Jack," she waved and called out, "Are you staying at the inn tonight?"

"Why?" he asked with a tone that was anything but friendly. Pearla was taken aback.

"Oh, sorry. I was just wondering." *No, there is no reason for this guy to be a jerk.*

"You know what, Jack? I've had a 'suboptimal' day." Pearla made exaggerated air quotes. "So, if you don't mind, forget I asked!"

She grabbed the burger from her car and slammed the door with more force than was necessary. Pearla didn't typically express her feelings in such a harsh manner, but her nerves felt raw, and even after two beers, she wasn't calm. The image of Jason Martinez's lifeless body in the ditch kept invading her mind.

Back inside, Max was asking Tyne if he could make time to visit the Worley property with them tomorrow.

"We'd like to explore it and snap some pictures, learn how it connects to the shore from the bluff. Would you know how to find any paths that lead down to the beach?"

Tyne nodded. "Sure, I know that property well. I mean, I used to. I went there many times as a kid. We'd explore every summer, even camped out a couple times. There were a number of trails. They were treacherous back then, so who knows if they're even functional now. That cliff has changed, too; it's never been stable. Basalt breaks off frequently in the rain. We never cared about our safety back then, and thankfully no one got injured, at least not seriously." He smiled, showing off his dimples, and ran his fingers through his hair.

"Let's go early in the morning. We'll be less likely to run into anyone," Pearla said.

"This is strictly curiosity, right? You ladies wouldn't be investigating anything, would you?" His eyes narrowed playfully.

"Us? Never!" Max acted shocked. "We'll be sneaking in like everyone else who isn't supposed to be there."

"Right, so it's a plan. I'll meet you at seven-thirty in the public lot. We can park there and walk over. Less obvious."

"Oh, Tyne. You think of everything. We're not the only sleuths," Pearla joked, her mood brightening with the idea of trying to bring justice to at least one of the dead men.

Tyne went back to work, leaving the three friends to continue their conversation. Max explained how she and Misty had shown up at the golf course. All three brothers were there along with J.T. Fields, but not Jason Martinez. Now they knew why.

"I may have implied that I'm reconsidering purchasing," Misty said.

"And I told them we have a friend who's thinking of making an offer as well," Max said. "J.T. was the only one who questioned us. He thinks we're bluffing and trying to drive up the price. He even intimated that the brothers asked us to be there to trick him into believing there was going to be a bidding war. We just laughed at that. They were letting J.T. try out the course. It was giving me flashbacks of yesterday, and I kept seeing him getting taken out by a golf ball coming out of nowhere. That's when you called, so I made an excuse that I was needed at the inn and we left."

Pearla mulled this over, a thought forming that she wasn't able to put into words, yet. *I'm a lightweight. Two beers and I'm buzzed. I better have an iced tea before I drive.*

"If Jason Martinez was run off the road on purpose, do you think they'll catch the driver? Where exactly did it happen?" Misty asked.

"It was right before the split in the highway, so the driver might have gone towards Mirror Lake or into Brookhaven. I can't stop wondering if it was intentional. Was someone trying to take out Mr. Martinez by running him off the highway and leaving him for dead? What do we know about Jason Martinez? Besides, up until today, he was our prime suspect in the death of Bruce Taylor."

"Okay, but remember, we also don't know for certain Bruce Taylor was purposely killed with that golf ball. It could've been an accident," Max reminded her.

The thought of two strange deaths in two days, both involving men who were interested in purchasing a property that might forever alter the town of Silvermist Point, to Pearla, was not, could not, be coincidental.

"This was planned," she said louder than she meant to. "Someone doesn't want this development to happen."

Misty's eyes widened. "You really think so?"

"Pearla's right," Max agreed. "We need to get the neighborhood app on our phones. Then we can see the comments about the accident. Maybe someone witnessed it." Max asked Tyne to text her, Pearla, and Misty an invitation to join the app. You had to be a local resident and be invited in order to comment and see the posts. Once they downloaded the app and accepted the invitation, they could access the feed.

"The post about the accident is blowing up," Misty said. "And Silvermist is not that big. I didn't think there were enough people in this town who would even know how to use this app."

"It's cross-posted to Brookhaven, Mirror Lake, and Silvermist Bay. That's why there are so many comments," Pearla explained while skimming through them.

Photos showed the long black skid marks that stopped at the gravel next to the roadside drainage ditch. The driver was headed southbound and could have gone to Brookhaven and beyond or to the tiny town of Mirror

Lake, where the construction of Misty's wellness spa was underway. Maybe Jason Martinez was distracted and had veered too far into the car lane, but the skid marks told a different story. Could be the driver was distracted and had accidentally forced the cyclist off the road. Accident or not, the driver chose to leave the scene and neglected to call 911, which might have saved the victim's life.

* * *

Back at the inn, guests gathered in the living room, enjoying the thoughtfully provided snacks. While the adults enjoyed a complimentary glass of wine, the family with the teenage boys planned to roast marshmallows in the fire pit after dark. Larry offered to set it up and wait around to safely put out the flames.

"Thanks, Larry, we've got it. You can enjoy your evening," Max told him.

The guests carried on, thankfully unaware of the accident that had left a man dead. Apparently, the news hadn't reached anyone here, including J.T. Fields, who sat in one of the oversized chairs, staring at a book. This made sense if the guests had stayed on the property and had not ventured into town this afternoon. They would have no way of knowing. It would be on the news, though.

There was only one television at the inn, located in the living room. The individual rooms had never had TVs and Max didn't want that to change. If people really needed that distraction, she supposed they could use their laptops. Good luck with the weak guest Wi-Fi, though. In the closet, along with an absurd amount of board games, one could also find an extensive collection of movies on both

DVD and VHS. Anyone staying at the inn was free to use them and host a movie night in the living room.

Each guest room had a small refrigerator, so usually the guests ate dinner in the village or traveled to Brookhaven before settling in for the evening. Another option was Mama's Pizza. It served delicious Italian cuisine, and the staff was happy to deliver orders to the inn. Sometimes guests would ask to use the main kitchen, and this was fine, too, so long as they cleaned up after themselves.

Max and Pearla were learning the rhythms of the inn. It was its own small ecosystem and functioned best when they listened first and made decisions only with careful consideration. Pearla suspected Amelia, the resident ghost, had much to do with this. Amelia was so familiar to the inn, it was as if she was a part of it.

"Amelia isn't allowing guests to know what happened," Pearla said confidently. "She's keeping them in the safe bubble of the inn. Did you notice the Mama's Pizza menu on the table in the living room? I didn't put it there. She doesn't want the guests to go into the village."

"Amelia, help us figure out what to do," Max pleaded under her breath just as Pearla got the alert for the reception desk and touched her phone screen to see the camera.

"It must be Nolan Briggs."

They'd been expecting the fourth guest and potential investor hosted by the Worley brothers.

"I'll check him in. Hopefully, he came straight here and hasn't heard the news about Jason Martinez."

Pearla greeted Nolan Briggs in reception with a smile and an outstretched hand. His grip was firm, but his hand felt moist and sweaty, and after shaking, Pearla wiped her hand on her jeans surreptitiously. The man was short and plump with a receding hairline and the dregs of a wispy mustache. His white golf shirt was too sheer and strained to contain his midsection. For a moment, Pearla mused at how different the potential investors were. Jason Martinez was fit and good-looking. J.T. Fields was tall and imposing with a superior air about him, and Bruce Taylor had looked like a middle-aged dad that coached his kid's soccer team. Interesting how the wealthy presented themselves.

"Is this lot secure?" Nolan Briggs sniffed, pointing his weak chin in the direction of the inn's gravel parking lot. "My truck is important to me, it's customized and I've put a lot of money into it."

"Absolutely, it's secure." Pearla bristled. Her ex-boyfriend, whom she desperately tried never to think about, had obsessed over his truck and it had annoyed her no end during their entire relationship. Who cared what kind of car or truck you drove? She couldn't help but ask, "Are you from Los Angeles?" To her, this would explain his paranoia and pompous attitude.

"Yes, why do you ask?"

Pearla thought quickly. "Just wondering if you enjoyed the drive up. That's quite a haul. You'll find it's a much slower pace here in Silvermist Point. It takes a bit of getting used to, but I believe you'll find the change of pace peaceful."

"Hmm, good to know. Can I get checked in, please? I'm beat. Too tired to go get dinner. I plan to veg out in front of the television, and sleep in 'til my appointment tomorrow."

"Oh, there aren't any TVs in the rooms," Pearla blurted. "But we've got an impressive reading collection. Books for every taste, and you're welcome to borrow one. Or you could relax in the hot tub, or sit out by the fire pit." *Shut up, Pearla.*

"Thanks, that's a lot of information. I appreciate it." A moment of silence passed before Pearla held up the old-fashioned brass key and offered to show him to his room. He followed behind her, rolling his suitcase and carrying a second large backpack over his shoulder. They passed through the living room, where the family was eating pizza and salad at the long dining table.

"There's an idea," Nolan said. "I can order a pizza."

"Mama's Pizza is the best," Pearla said.

"You'll find the number in the binder in your room. And I'm happy to pour you a glass of red wine if you like. It's from the local winery. You missed the wine and cheese reception. We host a little gathering for our guests every afternoon."

"No wine, thanks. I've brought my own." He patted his luggage.

"Sure, okay. The room is just this way." Pearla took the stairs, and Nolan followed. They arrived at the door and Pearla stepped aside, handing off the key.

"I should let you know I'm married." *Oh, my goodness. He thinks I was coming on to him!*

"Whoa, no. You've misunderstood. I'm only trying to make you feel comfortable here." Insulted, she fast-walked to the stairs, eager to get away.

"I'll leave you to it," she called out. *Max is gonna laugh so hard when I tell her this.*

Chapter 11

Was it disrespectful to snoop into the rooms of the two deceased guests? Max and Pearla thought not. After all, they needed to collect the personal effects of the two men for their loved ones, didn't they? And the rooms needed to be cleaned. No one was snooping, per se. Pearla carried two large tote bags printed with the inn's logo to gather up items. They took the exterior stairs and entered Mr. Martinez's second-floor room first, using the master key. His room was next to J.T. Fields, while Bruce Taylor and Nolan Briggs were staying in the other two upstairs rooms across the courtyard.

The curtains were closed, and Max flipped the switch for the overhead light. The ancient chandelier was for looks, not illumination. Several floor lamps served that purpose. The queen bed was made, not to Max's standards, but the fact it was made at all gave her a glimpse into the man's personality. She was a firm believer in making your bed as the way to begin your day on the right path. Unfortunately, not today. Rest in peace, Jason Martinez. Both women slipped on plastic cleaning gloves.

A closed laptop sat on the desk, and next to it, a file folder. Pearla picked it up and spread the papers over the desk. The heading read, "Worley Property." She scanned it.

"It's a printed email exchange. And here's an overhead shot of the property."

Max peered over Pearla's shoulder at the pages, squinting. Pearla noticed a pair of cheap magnifying half-glasses on the desk and handed them to her.

"That's better. I should probably face the fact that I need these if I expect to see anything up close. It's time to get one of those beaded necklaces, so I can have them close at all times."

Pearla began carefully taking a photo of each paper before returning it to the file folder. Guilt poked at Max. *Is this a violation of privacy?*

They gathered the few pants and shirts hanging in the closet and a plastic bag of dirty laundry from the floor. A quick sweep of the bathroom turned up only a toiletry kit: toothbrush, floss, comb, razor, deodorant and a prescription bottle of blood pressure pills. He traveled light.

Pearla folded and placed the clothes and bathroom kit into the suitcase, and put the papers and laptop in the shoulder bag. "We can store this in the office and ask Rene what we should do with it. He might want to take it down to the station in Brookhaven."

One more quick visual sweep of the room turned up nothing, and Max quietly shut the door.

"Alright, let's search Bruce Taylor's room next," Pearla said.

"You mean respectfully gather his belongings."

"Yes, that's what I mean."

The room was similar to the one they'd just left. Queen bed, desk and chair, small sitting area and restroom. Housekeeping had made Bruce's bed on the day he died; this was evident by the clean towels and throw pillows perfectly placed. He had to have made the request for service specifically. *He's fastidious. Or was.* For guests staying the week, rooms were freshened daily only if specifically requested, while towels and linens were changed every third day.

Several pairs of golf shorts and shirts hung in the free-standing armoire closet, as well as pants and a light jacket. Max began to remove each piece and when she came to the jacket, stuck her hand first in one pocket, then the other. Nothing. She folded the clothing and set it on the bed, dragged the empty suitcase over and loaded the clothes in. She shoved the shoes into the laundry bag and set them on top. "Find anything in the bathroom or the desk?"

Pearla was sitting at the desk flipping through a day planner. "The laptop's locked, so no help there. This day planner is written in shorthand or something. Nothing stands out. Here's a note for yesterday's appointment, and when I go back a few days, there's a phone number. It says AW with an 805 number. I'm taking a photo."

Max flipped through the planner once more from the beginning to the current date. *Was that my name I just saw?* She turned the pages more slowly and stopped on a page where 'Maxine Egan SPI' and the inn's phone number were written.

"Look here." She turned the date book toward Pearla and pointed. "This is from nearly two months ago. Pearla, when did Pete Worley book the rooms for the investors?"

"Not two months ago, more like two weeks ago. This must have been in the works longer than we realized."

"Were all the men contacted this early, do you think? I wonder if the property was ever listed for sale publicly?"

Max hadn't used a real estate agent for her purchase of the inn. It was sold directly to her from the previous owners. She'd had a real estate lawyer look over the deal and had secured a loan for the amount she couldn't pay upfront.

The Worley brothers might be doing the same, handling the sale themselves and not advertising the property too widely. Why, though? Could the four men staying at the inn be in such competition and want this particular piece of land so badly that they'd kill for it?

Chapter 12

Tuesday
Maxine

It's open," Max shouted from the kitchen when she heard a tapping on the wooden door of her cottage. She laughed when Pearla met her in her kitchen lugging a twenty-pound cream tabby cat.

"Come here, Naughty," she said as Butters was deposited into her arms. He had taken to wandering lately, but thankfully was always within shouting distance and could be relied upon to hear his treats being shaken from miles away.

"I made you a cappuccino. Where was this guy? I hope he wasn't bothering guests."

"Nope. He was outside my door, so I thought I'd bring

him over." Pearla sipped her cappuccino. "He seems to know which guests are cat people and who needs to be won over. I saw Larry bend down to give him a scratch when he thought no one was looking. It was sweet."

"We should head over. I don't want to keep Tyne waiting," Max said.

"I bet you don't," Pearla smirked and batted her eyelashes. "Emma's taking care of the breakfast spread today, so we can take off whenever you're ready." They quickly drank their coffee and left to meet Tyne.

When Max pulled the car into the unmarked gravel parking lot, Tyne was already there waiting. He was wearing low hiking boots today, rather than his usual leather flip flops, and had a small backpack. Next to him stood a brown, medium-sized dog, tail wagging enthusiastically and straining on the leash to greet them.

"This is Chief. He belongs to my parents. I've offered to take him off their hands for a while. I don't think they knew what they were in for when they adopted him. He's a good boy, a shepherd mix, just has a lot of energy and needs some training. The agency said he was three years old, but I suspect he's younger and still a puppy."

"He's darling!" Pearla gushed as she squatted down to greet him, allowing him to lick her face. "Hi, Chief."

"So cute!" Max bent down to offer Chief a pet. "Sorry we're a little late."

"You're not late," Tyne said. "I've only been here a few minutes. I drove around to locate the best place to enter. Follow me, ladies."

They walked along the fencing until Tyne pointed out where it had been cut and pulled back. He stepped through first with Chief before holding a hand out to assist Max, then Pearla. The air was damp and cool with a low-hanging mist. This quiet, peaceful atmosphere was one of the qualities that drew people to Silvermist Point and begged some to settle here or at least return many times. *I belong here. I came back so many times until Silvermist Point called me home to stay. I wonder what Tyne's story is. How did he end up here?*

"I heard they planned to repair the perimeter fencing again, but they've done it before only to have people figure a way in. Everyone local knows it's abandoned and unguarded. And it's an unspoken agreement that we all just let it be. Even Sheriff Silva doesn't patrol this area," Tyne said, and guided them through the brush until they reached the front of the property. Chief's tail wagged nonstop and his nose was to the ground, enjoying the scents.

Tyne said he wasn't sure about letting Chief off the leash. The dog had escaped his parents' yard twice, so he didn't trust him not to take off. "Let's start here and work our way to the bluff."

The acreage that was once a nine-hole golf course was still recognizable, especially the area the Worley brothers had restored, along with the burned-out remains of the clubhouse and what used to be the parking lot. The asphalt in the lot was cracked, and grass and dandelions had sprouted up, but the majority of the property appeared as undeveloped coastal forest with overgrown trees, some dead and decomposing, with years of built-up needles and leaves on the ground, creating a pleasant earthy aroma as well as habitats for all kinds of small creatures.

"I'm unsure what we're hoping to find, if anything," Max said. "Yet, I think I'll know if I see it."

They continued through the cleared portion of the golf course and back into a denser part of the property. One could easily get lost here. Narrow pathways were everywhere, but they ran into each other and split off in all directions. After a couple minutes, a rustling from nearby bushes drew their attention, and by instinct, all three froze and peered around, their senses sharpened. A low growl rumbled in Chief's throat, and a stiff mohawk formed from the fur on his spine.

"Over there," Pearla whispered and pointed. Some mid-height bushes and undergrowth on the left moved.

"Probably a raccoon or squirrel, maybe a deer," Tyne said.

Max's eyes were trained on the bush where the sound had come from. The leaves rustled again and the long barrel of a rifle emerged. Max drew in a breath as her heart paused. *Someone is trying to kill us.*

Next, a pop from behind and something whizzing past her head, a splotch of blue exploding on the leaves in front of her, followed by a return shot from the bushes, resulting in bright red liquid finding its mark on a tree trunk.

"What the hell?" Tyne shouted. "Show yourselves!" Chief pranced and panted excitedly.

A moment of quiet and then two fully camouflaged figures emerged, one from the bushes with a rifle pointed at the ground, and the other from behind a thick-trunked tree. Both individuals blended so well with the surroundings, it was unnerving. *Are there more of them hiding?*

"We're just having a paintball war. Everyone does it. We didn't mean to scare you," a clearly male teenaged voice protested from behind his face covering. Tyne's hearty laugh echoed through the woods.

"Yeah, yeah, okay. You scared us though. Are you boys locals?"

"Sort of, and I'm not a boy," a clearly female voice said.

"You shouldn't assume."

"My apologies," Tyne assured as Max found her voice again.

"Mind if I ask you some questions about paintballing, now that I can breathe again? You gave me quite a scare." She made a show of clutching her chest. "Don't worry, your secret's safe with us. As you can see, we're trespassing too, so we're hardly going to report you."

"Alright. What did you want to know? Hold on a sec." The boy pulled his walkie-talkie from his vest and spoke into it. "Game paused. I repeat. Game paused. Over."

"Over," came the crackling response.

"There are only six of us today, three per team. I doubt you'll see them. They won't want to reveal their positions."

"Do you ever get injured from the paint bullets?" Max asked.

"Nah, we wear protective gear. You get used to the impact, even if the weapon's been modified. It hurts though," the boy said.

"Yup, lots of bruises when you first learn." There was an edge of pride in the girl's voice.

"So, you might have really hurt us. We don't have any protective gear," Pearla said.

"Impossible. Never would have happened. I was aiming for my opponent and I'm an excellent shot. I've got a scope," the boy bragged.

"Well, it sounds like a blast. I think I'd like to try paintballing," Tyne said. "Where do I get the equipment? Do I need a license or anything?"

"Nope, no license. Anyone can do it. There's a supply store in Brookhaven. You have to be eighteen to buy the bullets and weapons." There was no way these two kids were eighteen, but no one was going to call them out.

"Aren't there facilities to use instead of trespassing?" Pearla asked, then added, "Not that I'm judging you, just wondering. Not sure if you heard, but the owners are selling this property."

"Those places are too expensive. Too many rules. They don't allow weapon modifications. Here we can play by our own rules."

Max noticed they didn't comment on the owners selling the property. She wanted to keep them talking. "It'll be a real bummer when they sell it. I like to practice my golf swing here. I've never seen any paintballers in person, only the splotches of color. You guys sure know how to be stealthy."

"The paint's biodegradable. We don't harm anything," the girl said defensively. "Unlike the golfers who tear up the ground and litter the forest floor with their golf balls. They don't even bother to collect them. I've even seen them aim off the bluff straight into the ocean. That can't be good for marine life."

"Oh, I never leave my golf balls around," Max assured. "They're expensive."

"Speaking of golfers, did you hear about the man who was killed?" Pearla asked.

"No. Why would we?"

Why is she so defensive?

"Just thought I'd ask. It was an unfortunate accident. Tragic." There was a lull in the conversation, and everyone stood as if waiting.

"We'll be on our way. Would you mind asking the other players not to aim for us? Just let them know we're exploring the property. We'd appreciate it," Tyne said.

"Sure," said the boy. Max watched as he disappeared completely back into the bushes, and when she turned to watch the girl, she too had vanished.

"It's easy to disappear here, or not be seen if you don't want to be," Max said.

"Always has been," Tyne said.

"You know, there should have been a golf ball to find the day Bruce Taylor was killed. I keep thinking about it. Where was it? I wonder if someone grabbed it while we were all distracted," Pearla said. "It was in a wooded area, and now that I see how camouflaged the paintballers are…"

"If we found it, would it matter? What could they get from the golf ball anyway? It's not as if there'd be fingerprints on it," Max said.

"That's true, but it still bothers me we couldn't find it. So strange. Where could it have gone?"

"If you want, we can pass through the area where the guy was struck before we leave, give it another look," Tyne suggested, and Pearla agreed it would be a good idea. Max doubted they'd discover anything useful.

When they made it to the edge of the property, they stood on the bluff, just taking in the beauty of the vast ocean stretched out before them. The fog had dissipated, and the dark, endless blue of the ocean merged with the brighter blue sky. Max removed her light jacket and tied it around her waist. Tyne took off his flannel, revealing a black tank top.

"Breathtaking!" Max said, smiling. "This view never disappoints."

Pearla nudged her, and Max blushed, hoping Tyne wouldn't notice. The cliffs were ragged where pieces had eroded or broken off. They stayed a few feet back from the edge so that they couldn't see the beach directly below. Tyne offered to show them the trails he remembered.

"There are still a few folks who use the trails," he said. "But no one maintains them."

The first one they located was very rough and appeared unsafe. It could hardly be called a proper trail. Max could see that at one time there had been switchbacks, but it now looked too narrow to walk down and not as if anyone had used it lately. She was relieved when Pearla said, "I don't need to be breaking my leg. Can we not attempt this one?"

They walked further. The next trail was even more treacherous looking.

"Do you really think anyone uses these?" Max asked. She had hiked the trail from the public park on another part of the bluff and had been proud to survive. That trail was well-known among the residents and even boasted a warning sign to attempt it at your own risk. These had no signs because technically they weren't official trails at all. No one was supposed to be on this private property.

"We definitely used them as kids," Tyne said. "But that's when you're too foolhardy to care about things like your own well-being or safety." He laughed. "Let's keep walking and maybe we'll find another way down, a safer option."

"Yes, please," Max agreed. "I would imagine whoever buys this would want to install some sort of railing along the entire bluff. A safe staircase to the beach would be great, too."

"Even with railings in place, people can be morons. Every year visitors die by falling into the Grand Canyon," Pearla said. "Every. Single. Year. And it's always for a better shot; they don't want the railing to show in their photo."

Tyne stopped and pointed. "Ah, I think this is the one my friends and I used to use." The trail was more obvious than the others, but the difficulty level was concerning.

"There are fresh shoe prints," Pearla said. "Let's follow it down."

"If it's the one I remember, it'll lead to the beach where my friends and I hung out as teenagers. We had a cave we used to meet in and…" He trailed off.

"Get wasted, I assume," Pearla snickered. "Don't worry, Tyne, we won't think less of you for your childhood indiscretions. Especially me. I was something of a wild child back in the day."

"Pearla, you're still so young. How far back was 'back in the day' anyway?" Tyne teased.

"Far enough. And I'm in my thirties, Tyne."

Max was only half listening. Her mind dwelled on the comment about the cave. Could it be the same cave she and Char had discovered on one of their last visits to Silvermist Point? She'd thought about it a few times since moving here and had intended to search for it just to know if it was still there, but she'd been so busy with learning how to run the inn. Plus, she wanted Char there, too.

"How old are you, Tyne?" *Great, Max, that wasn't too direct or anything.*

"I'm fifty-five," Tyne said without hesitation.

That lines up. He looks way younger.

"Oh, sorry to just blurt that out." Max took a breath before continuing. "Now I owe you my age. It's fifty-one. Just turned."

It felt good to say it. Max was sick of being concerned about other people judging her. When Char had turned fifty, she'd accepted it and even celebrated with an elaborate party, but had proclaimed, "This is it. No more birthdays for me. I shall remain fifty." And fifty she was for anyone who asked, even while Max, her same-age best friend, had advanced to fifty-one.

"Char and I found a cave when we were girls. It occurred to me, we might be talking about the same one, that's why I asked how old you are. We searched for it when we learned the story about Amelia and how her love waited for her there."

Tyne raised his eyebrows.

"Are you familiar with the story?" Max asked. She had filled Pearla in when Amelia had first made herself known, but she hadn't had time to research the history of the inn, including the Amelia legend, any further and was curious if Tyne had heard of the ghost.

"I only knew Amelia disappeared as a girl and was assumed dead, but her body was never found. And it's believed her spirit stays on at the inn. Wait, so you've seen her ghost?" he asked.

"Depends how you define ghost. It's her, though. Hard to explain, but she's … made herself known," Max said, trying her best to explain what she didn't understand well herself.

"She protects the inn, is what I believe," Pearla added, then changed the subject. "Let's find that cave."

They began their descent down the cliffside. Chief took the lead with the sure-footed confidence his human companions lacked. The dog appeared fearless and ready for adventure, tail wagging furiously and his lips pulled back, a doggy smile on his face. His canine confidence was comforting. *If Chief is not afraid, I won't be either.*

Tyne followed Chief on the one-person path, constantly turning back around to ensure he'd be prepared to catch Max or Pearla if they slipped. Max noticed and appreciated his concern. Once they got used to it, they gained confidence, pausing often to remark on the view.

Max could hear the sound of water, possibly a small creek, but wasn't able to see it through the thick vegetation growing from the cliffside. This path was well concealed and would be easily missed if you weren't paying attention or specifically trying to find a way down to the beach. Even the owners of properties on the bluffs had to use the public trail to get to the beach from one of the inlets, unless they installed a private staircase. The Snowy Plover Inn, however, was ideally located between two high bluffs, which made it the perfect location to access the beach.

When the shore was in sight, Max was flooded with relief that she'd made it, but was not looking forward to scrambling her way back up. The creek she heard revealed itself as a little waterfall that spilled onto a part of the cliff face and landed on the sand before flowing out to the ocean. It would provide a perfect marker to find your way back to the upward path, which was tricky to spot from the shore.

"How close are we to the inn?" Pearla mused. "The other day I saw footprints in the sand coming from this direction, then they disappeared."

"Hard to say, maybe a couple of miles. Could be less. Or more." Tyne's comment was not helpful.

The cliffs were so high; it was easy to see how someone could lose their way and get disoriented unless they knew the area well. The only option was to choose a direction and keep walking while hoping the tide wouldn't reach the base of the cliff. No matter how skinny, there was almost always a path along the cliffs, and if you just kept walking, you would either find a trail leading back up, or eventually an inlet leading out. From an aerial view, you could see the dips where the cliffs came apart with the valleys in the middle.

Silvermist Point reminded Max of the famously known Big Sur with its craggy coastline hugging steep cliff-sides interspersed with open meadows and redwood forests. Max thought of Silvermist Point as a smaller, more intimate version of Big Sur. But, unlike Big Sur, Silvermist had a little, central village. Still, it was often passed by as travelers continued to the bigger cities and popular beaches southward or the small, but more well-known destinations to the north.

Max and Pearla removed their shoes and socks as if by instinct, and curled their toes into the sand. Max couldn't stand to walk on the beach in shoes, even if it meant sand rubbing between her toes on the way back. She smiled when she saw Tyne do the same.

"I'm afraid I only have an hour or so more," Tyne said. "We'll need thirty minutes to get back up, so if you want to check for the golf ball, we're gonna need to leave here soon. There's not much time to search for the cave."

"That's okay, we can walk out from the inn another day," Max suggested, agreeing they should begin heading back soon. Going up might take twice as long as going down, and she hoped her leg muscles were up for the challenge, not that she'd complain or show any sign of being out of shape in front of Tyne.

Pearla pulled a bag of trail mix from her backpack, and the three ate handfuls and drank from their water bottles.

Tyne gave Chief a piece of jerky and a drink in a foldable fabric water bowl he'd brought. Large pieces of driftwood made perfect makeshift seating, while they took a moment to catch their breath and refuel.

"I'll take the lead after Chief," Tyne offered, easily pulling himself up onto the first section of steep trail. Max followed behind, then Pearla. The climb up was slower and more difficult. Foot placement was everything, as was finding the low branches to grab to assist in hoisting yourself up. Strenuous as it was, Max found the ascent even more invigorating than the climb down. It felt good to push herself, and the higher up she got, the more satisfying the view of the endless ocean became, as well as her sense of accomplishment.

When the small group reached the top, they stood on the flat surface and once again caught their breath and paused for a water break. Max scanned the area, wondering if she'd spot any more paintballers, but she saw nothing and heard only the whisper of the breeze in the trees and bushes.

"I did it," she said to no one in particular.

"I never doubted you could," Tyne said with a smile. "Though I wasn't sure about myself."

"Yeah, right," Pearla joked. "Let's have another look for the golf ball before we leave. Couldn't hurt."

Tyne scratched behind Chief's ears and down his back. "Chief's been such a good boy. Do you suppose we can trust him off the leash?"

"He's gotta be tired. He won't run away; he knows where the beef jerky is," Max said.

Tyne unclipped the leash, and the dog ran ahead, but dutifully checked in each time he was called, proving he could handle his increased freedom. When they reached the area of the incident, Chief began sniffing all around, and making shallow digs with his front paws.

"If only he could speak," Pearla said as she and the others walked the area looking closely at the ground.

"If there was a golf ball, we'd have found it," Max said. "Didn't we already do this on Monday?"

"Come on, boy. Here, Chief," Tyne called and held up the leash. Chief trotted back dutifully like a good boy.

"What's he got in his mouth?" Pearla patted the dog's head and held her other hand under his chops. "Drop it." Chief widened his jaws and deposited a camouflaged golf ball into Pearla's outstretched hand, panting and wagging his tail proudly.

"Why would anyone golf with this?" Tyne asked.

"Hmm," Max said. "First, they weren't using it for golfing. Second, they didn't want it found."

"Yup. Someone used this gag gift as their weapon. This had to be planned," Pearla said.

"What now? Will you call Sheriff Silva?" Tyne's expression was hard to decipher.

"I want to wait on that," Pearla said, speaking quickly and catching Max's eye. "We should discuss it first. Right, Max?" Max nodded, not sure why Pearla was hesitant to tell Rene about their find.

"You're good with that?" she asked.

"I'm not getting in the way of your investigation; you do what you gotta do," he said. "But I will say that I think you're right, even if I doubted it before. There is no way Bruce Taylor's death was a freak accident."

Chapter 13

Pearla

Pearla was busy settling accounts for the inn while trying to give her brain a break from thinking about the two dead men when a tap sounded on the half-open office door, interrupting her concentration.

"One sec," she said before scooting her wheeled office chair away from her desk and glancing over. Colby Trawl stood in the doorway, disheveled as always.

"May I come in?" he asked politely. *Since when have you ever used the words, "May I?"*

"Sure. How can I help you, Colby?" Pearla asked in an equally formal tone. Colby stepped in and sat stiffly in one of the chairs facing her. He pointed to the corner where the belongings of Bruce Taylor and Jason Martinez were stacked.

"Did you take that stuff from the dead guys' rooms?"

Pearla was taken aback. "Yes, we removed the contents of those rooms so they could, uh, be collected by the family members of the deceased." She tried to keep any guilty feelings from her tone. *What do you want, Colby? Why are you asking me this?*

"While you and Max were gone, another man who's staying here asked me to let him into this office."

"Which man?" Pearla interrupted.

"A short, fat one. He offered me a one hundred dollar bill to open the door and walk away." Colby stared at her. Pearla kept her voice smooth and calm with great effort.

"And did you?" she asked.

"Yeah. I took the money." *Stay calm, Pearla.*

"Colby, did you let him into my office?"

"Nope, of course not. You know I can't open this door. You changed the locks. But I told him I could, and I took the money." A self-satisfied expression crossed his face. "Then I faked trying to open it and said my key wouldn't work. The guy was pissed off, but what do I care?"

"Oh, thank you." Pearla's words stumbled out. "I'd forgotten you don't have a key."

Colby furrowed his brows. *Is he angry?* "I'm telling you, I wouldn't have let him in even if I did have a key. You should trust me."

Pearla momentarily wondered if Colby might actually be helpful. She pictured his collection of paintballing equipment.

"We trust you, Colby. I hope you know that." Pearla let that sink in for a moment, then added, "Max and I aren't convinced Bruce Taylor died accidentally. We think someone killed him."

Colby's expression remained neutral, as if he heard this

kind of news every day. "And the other guy?"

"Same," Pearla said and waited for a reaction. Colby raised his eyebrows, but said nothing in response. After an uncomfortable silence, Pearla claimed she needed to get back to work and thanked him again for his honesty and for letting her know what happened. *I'll see what Max thinks.* Careful to lock the door behind her, Pearla set off to find Max.

"I'm still not sure about Colby," Max said. "I mean, look how quick he was to take that man's money." She paused. "Pearla, you don't think he'd accept a payment to kill someone, do you?" Then Max answered her own question in a one-sided conversation. "No. There is no way."

"Max, think about it. Colby had no reason to tell me about the transaction. I believe he was trying to be helpful in his own way. He's definitely not bright enough to inform me just to throw us off his trail."

"Yeah, that's true," Max agreed.

"We could try to pick his brain about paintballing…" Pearla suggested, again calling to mind the horde of equipment she'd stumbled upon at the Trawl house.

"Let's keep that option in our back pocket for now," Max said.

"I think the bigger concern is that creep, Nolan Briggs. He wanted access to our office. That makes him a suspect," Pearla said.

"True, but I think our next move is to speak with the Worley siblings. They'll have vetted the investors, certainly, and must have thoughts on two of them turning up dead. Plus, they think Char wants to make an offer, so we have a perfect excuse to talk with them without them thinking we're fishing."

* * *

Max pulled into the pockmarked asphalt driveway at the Worley family property. No other cars were present, but one or more might be parked inside the attached three-car garage. The A-frame home was a deluxe version of a mountain lodge. The forest-green paint blended well with the surroundings, but it was peeling and needed a fresh coat. Even in its state of disrepair, the Worley family home was beautiful. So much potential, but it had been neglected over the years. As Tyne had said, no one used it anymore.

They took the stairs from the driveway and crossed the wooden deck. Arriving at the front door, Pearla pressed the rusted doorbell. When she heard nothing, she knocked tentatively, then with more force while calling, "Anyone home?" No answer.

She peeked in the narrow window panel next to the door. No lights were on inside, but she could see into the front room. A large L-shaped couch dominated the space and faced the fireplace. The connected kitchen had dishes piled on the counters and an overflowing trashcan. Max knocked more forcefully. Still no answer.

"Let's walk around the back," Max said. "I don't think anyone's here."

Behind the home, needles from several imposing pines littered the ground, and the wooden fencing around the yard was rotted and falling down. Max pointed at smudges of powdery blue and red color on the trunks of the trees.

"Looks like the Worley brothers are paintballers, too. Whoever knew it was so popular?" Pearla said, while noticing the Worley home was quite isolated; she figured it was likely the Worleys owned much of the surrounding land. The only neighbors were far down the steep block.

"I'd like to speak with someone who knew the Worley parents, and the siblings when they were younger. Who are the old timers? Have we met any of them at one of the town meetings? Anyone who won't think we're prying if we ask questions?" Pearla said.

Though they had made some close friends, Max and Pearla were still the newbies in town and, as such, many of the locals were wary of them.

"How about Mr. O'Leary? He seems friendly enough, and he's really old. He must've known the family back in the day," Max said. "Janice is a good bet too. She knows everything about everyone."

"And having The Post Stop right next to the sheriff helps too," Pearla said. "We should make friends with her."

"That might be easier said than done, though. Janice loves to stir the pot and share gossip, but only on her terms. Discretion isn't her strong suit."

"Right," Pearla agreed, remembering it was Janice who had dropped the bomb about Beth's death, even before Larry knew. Thinking of that uncomfortable scene reminded her of the file boxes she and Max had cleared from the Trawls.

"Max, the boxes from the Trawls. They could be a veritable treasure trove of information. We've got to go through them." She and Max had intended to peruse the old copies of the *Silvermist Point of View* newsletters from the box they'd kept, as well as sort through the other box, which at first glance appeared to be scraps of gathered information on residents of Silvermist Point, but they had not found the time yet.

"I can't believe we haven't dug into that yet," Max said. "It's a good place to start. There's no reason to stay here if no one's around to speak with us."

Pearla agreed. As they pulled away, she thought she saw an upstairs curtain flutter. *Was someone home and had purposely ignored them? Why?*

* * *

Back at the cottage, Max set up the stovetop espresso pot on one burner, and a stainless steel pitcher of milk on the other and turned the heat on low. On the long wooden table, where Pearla had shooed Butters from his nap, she dumped the contents of the extra file box they'd taken from Beth Trawl's closet. Butters arranged himself into a cat loaf on the bench seat next to her.

"I figured I'd dump it," Pearla called out to Max. "This may appear to be a file box, but these are anything but. Just a collection of scraps we'll need to pick through to make any sense of." She spread out the various-sized scraps in the same way one might spread out the pieces when starting a new puzzle, but there was no clear way to begin. Max joined her and helpfully suggested they start with looking for anything related to the Worleys.

"Good idea," Pearla agreed. "Most of these have names and dates at the top. That'll be useful."

Max held up a tiny spiral notepad. "I noticed there are a few of these so I'll make a pile for them. I'll bet Beth carried them in her purse to record stuff on a day-to-day basis. Listen to this…" Max flipped to a random page and read the date and entry aloud. "John Perkins, 3 pm, corner booth in Mama's Pizza—conversing with an unknown woman—not his wife—crosscheck info."

"So nosy!" Pearla remarked. "I wonder if John Perkins,

whoever he is, was having an affair."

"We do need to remember, these notes were only for Beth's eyes. She wasn't counting on anyone rifling through them after her death," Max said.

"For that matter, she wasn't counting on dying at all," Pearla said as she held up a crumpled paper, then smoothed it on the tabletop. "This is a medical summary. It's a diagnosis of terminal cancer. Peter Worley Senior. He had cancer. Did we know that, Max?"

"No, we did not. Larry told me Pete died when he fell down the stairs. And his body wasn't found for weeks." Max shuddered. "Larry never mentioned cancer."

"Maybe Larry didn't know. It could've been a secret." Pearla examined the form more closely and read the handwritten note at the bottom: Taken from the trash bin at the store (MG).

"Look at this! Read what Beth wrote at the bottom." Pearla thrust the paper at Max.

"So, she fetched it out of the garbage of Miscellaneous Goods. That's bold," Max said.

"Right? I'm shredding my personal paperwork from now on," Pearla said.

"Don't you already? Just to be safe?"

"No. I never imagined anyone taking it out of the trash, or caring what it said."

"Okay, back to business. Do you suppose his kids knew he had cancer?" Max let the question hang as she went to the kitchen to prepare the coffees. Pearla pondered the revelation that Pete Worley Senior had been gravely ill when he died. The autopsy report would indicate accidental death since he fell down the stairs. Hmm, I wonder if Rene could get a copy.

When Max returned with the coffees and two buttermilk scones, Pearla lowered her mug down to Butters, allowing him to lick the foam. Then she broke off a small piece of scone and fed it to him from her palm. "Little King," she cooed and gave him a pet.

"He is getting too plump!" Max laughed. "Butters, you are spoiled." The cat's purrs grew louder as if to say, "Don't I know it."

Both women rummaged through the pile for a few minutes. It was easy to get distracted by the fascinating bits and scraps of receipts mixed with handwritten notes. Each one taken by itself, might not mean much—just a random scrap from someone's day-to-day life—but Pearla knew that if she could only piece together the right bits, a story would emerge and possibly provide answers related to the two recent deaths in Silvermist.

How? She couldn't decipher yet, but there was a story here. Many stories. And she was thankful they hadn't been quick to toss the box and all its contents in the dumpster when they'd sorted through Beth's personal items.

Pearla stopped sorting when something caught her eye. "This is a receipt from the post office. Annie Worley has a P.O. box. Or did."

Chapter 14

Sheriff Rene Silva

Sheriff Rene Silva agreed to meet with Pearla and Max, not because he believed they had anything in the way of pertinent information regarding the cases of Bruce Taylor or Jason Martinez, rather because he enjoyed their company. They were two of the people he most wanted to actually be friends with in the town. In short, he admired them, especially Pearla, whom he fantasized had a secret crush on him. She was easy on the eyes and her spunky personality was a breath of fresh air in his otherwise rather humdrum life. He would never ask her out though, for fear of the lingering awkwardness if she were to decline. So, for now, friends.

"We'll be at your office in ten minutes," Pearla said.

And sure enough, she peeked through the door ten minutes later with Max behind her.

"Come in." Rene stood and gestured toward the fold-out chairs provided for guests. His office was bare bones. Rene suspected it had been a storage closet in a former life. He'd hung his framed credentials from the police academy behind his desk using push-pins in the soft plaster. A locking file cabinet with a single-cup coffee maker atop it, a wobbly bookcase crammed with God-knows-what, and a small dorm-sized fridge filled the space. The walls were a depressing gray that had once been white, and the small window was half covered in bent metal mini blinds. Rene could use the main police station in Brookhaven to complete his reports, but he appreciated a dedicated workspace in Silvermist Point, even if it lacked proper privacy and had zero prestige. Max set a paper plate covered in wax paper on the edge of his desk, and the scent of sugar and cinnamon wafted into the cramped space. Both women sat.

"Snickerdoodles," Max said. "Marjory taught me the recipe. She learned it from Mable, before the Evanses retired. I'm still practicing."

"Well, they smell amazing." Rene found a napkin on the bookshelf and grabbed a cookie, taking a bite without hesitating, then moaning appreciatively. "Max, I think you've mastered it." He polished off the rest of the cookie in a second bite, wiped crumbs from his mouth and asked, "So, to what do I owe the pleasure?"

"We want to ask about the..." Pearla leaned in close and whispered, "murders." Max cocked her head toward the open door before getting up to close it firmly.

Good thinking, Max. Janice will one hundred percent try to listen in.

Rene kept his voice low. "As you're aware, I can't speak freely about investigations or open cases. That being said, if you have any information you think might be elucidating, fire away." Rene pulled the pen from behind his ear and clicked it, then flipped to a fresh sheet of yellow legal paper, where he scrawled the date at the top.

"I'll go first," Pearla offered. "We had a strong hunch Jason Martinez was the one responsible for Bruce Taylor's death. Avid golfer, proven interest in acquiring the property, and no solid alibi when the death occurred, but we all know it couldn't have been him."

Rene acknowledged this statement with a solemn nod. Max spoke next.

"So now we have two dead men, both of whom were staying at our inn."

"And you think the deaths of these men are related?" Rene asked.

"Don't you?" Pearla said, and without waiting for a response, went on. "So, we're back to motive. Who profits from their deaths? As I see it, either one of the remaining two other investors, by improving their odds of securing the deal. One of the brothers, for reasons we're not sure of, since they are in agreement to sell. Or someone else, maybe with a desire to leave the property as-is." She paused and took a breath.

"Off the record," Rene paused. "I also suspected Jason Martinez initially. And it's not beyond the realm of possibility that he killed Bruce Taylor, and then was subsequently killed by accident. That assumes a lot of coincidence, though." *Am I making any sense? Talking too much?*

"Have any tips come in, or witnesses who might have

seen something? Has Martinez's death been declared an accident?" Pearla's face had doubt written all over it.

"He was not struck by a vehicle. That has been determined. His fatal injuries were sustained when he crashed into the drainage ditch."

"But the skid marks! There were skid marks. I saw them," Pearla said.

"Yes, there were skid marks. However, the vehicle that caused them made no contact with the victim. That's not to say someone didn't force him off the road and ultimately cause the accident, but without a witness…"

"There's no proof," Max said, then threw a verbal curveball. "On a related subject, where is the Worley sister in all of this? Her name is Annie, and all we know about her is that she went off the grid years ago and hasn't been heard from since."

How do they know about Annie?

Rene focused on keeping his expression neutral. "Evidently, she's been gone longer than seven years, so the brothers don't need her consent to sell. For that reason, she's not a concern." Rene leaned back in his chair, looking from one to the other as if to say, "What else you got?"

"We know she has a P.O. Box here in Silvermist. Is it active? Does she have her mail forwarded? Was her disappearance suspicious at all, or out of character at the time?"

"Good questions, Pearla." Rene scribbled some illegible notes, giving himself a moment to process. *How do they know she has a P.O. box?*

"Can you ask Janice about the P.O. box? If it's inactive, then it's a dead end. If not, maybe we, or you, should try to reach out to Annie Worley." Pearla looked into his eyes, no doubt expecting an answer. Instead, he posed a question.

"How did you come by the information that Annie has a P.O. box, or even that she's a fourth sibling? You're new to town, and she's been gone for years."

"We have our sources," Pearla said slyly while tucking an unruly curl behind her ear. "And we're willing to collaborate."

Rene made a snap decision to share what he knew. "Janice already told me that Annie Worley had renounced her place in the family before her father died. She sent messages to everyone who knew her that she was leaving Silvermist to live a life of poverty, going off the grid, and not to contact her. She said she wanted no part of the family's wealth; her brothers could have it all."

"Strange. Why would she do that?" Max mused.

"Janice claims Annie was always an oddball. Maybe it stemmed from being the lone girl in a family full of boys. Supposedly, she was quite wild in her teen years, and in her twenties, she dated very wealthy and much older men, but she never married. She rarely returned to Silvermist at all over the years until the father, Pete Senior, gathered his children at his home to discuss his vision for the family land. Apparently, there was some kind of family feud, and Annie renounced her place in the family and took off to lead a life of austerity on her own terms. She planned to start fresh and cut all ties. She didn't come back for her dad's funeral even, just sent her condolences and a wreath to the church."

"Janice told you all this information?" Max asked.

"Correct. Janice knows it all. She's the eyes and ears of this town." Both women nodded in agreement.

"Has anyone seen or heard from Annie recently, or

even in the last few years?" Pearla asked.

"Annie's in contact with Janice." Whoops. He hadn't planned to tell them that. Pearla sat up straighter and Rene imagined the wheels turning in her mind with this information.

"So, get her contact information and question her. She might know something," Pearla said, her voice rising with excitement.

"I'm sure you're not telling me how to do my job," Rene said, mildly insulted. "But I'll look into that angle."

"Will you let us know what you find out?" Max pressed. Before he answered, Pearla set a camouflaged golf ball on the desk between them.

"We believe this is the murder weapon used on Bruce Taylor." Rene picked it up.

"Where'd this come from?"

"We found it on the course when we went back there after Jason Martinez turned up dead. We don't like that these deaths are connected to the inn, so we're trying to figure out what's going on. Just wanted to help out. It must be challenging having to do it all alone."

Is she batting her eyelashes at me? He hoped so.

"I'll take this in as evidence." He reached for the golf ball. "Too bad it's been contaminated." Pearla picked up the ball and dropped it into his outstretched hand.

"I'd have collected this more carefully to preserve it, but as it was, I fetched it out of a dog's mouth, so if there was ever any DNA on it, that's been destroyed."

Chapter 15

Max

On the way out of Rene's office, Max and Pearla paused at the counter of the post office to make small talk with Janice. Max knew full well Janice had likely had her ear pressed to the adjoining door connecting the post office to the makeshift sheriff's office, trying to eavesdrop. Max infused her smile with sincerity before she spoke.

"Hi Janice. How are you?"

"Fine. And you?" Janice responded curtly.

"Pearla and I were just speaking with Sheriff Silva in his office."

As we both know you are aware. Max studied Janice's expression.

"We're concerned about the accident on the highway

and we hoped he'd have some information."

"Especially because the man who died was staying at the Snowy Plover Inn," Pearla added. Janice's expression was hard to read. She either wanted to bust out with all kinds of gossip, or was going to play coy.

"Yes, I'm aware of the accident. Horrible. Your inn sure seems to be having a streak of misfortune."

She's enjoying this.

"How do you mean?" Pearla asked innocently. "Are you referring to that silly gossip newsletter calling us 'The Hotel of Death'? A bit exaggerated, don't you think?" Janice's lips formed a tight line.

"We thought the newsletter had stopped. But then, there it was. Like magic." Max snapped her fingers for effect and watched Janice's expression closely for tells. "Any idea who writes it?" She let the question hang for a few seconds. "No matter. What I really wanted to do was invite you to lunch sometime." Now there was a clear shift as Janice's expression merged from skeptical to surprised.

"Oh, really? I'd like that. I'm kind of a one-woman show here, but I can get away for a quick bite. Let's plan it."

Max removed a business card from her purse and slid it across the counter. "That's my personal cell number on the back. You can text me with a day that works." They left a smiling Janice and walked out onto the street.

"Keep your friends close, and your enemies closer," Pearla said and nudged Max.

"I don't want her as an enemy, that's for sure. I almost mentioned we have copies of all the SMPOV newsletters from the last twenty-five years, but then she'll know that we know Beth was the author, or one of them."

"She's gotta be the other one. Who else?"

"Yeah, it's her. Gotta be. But let's play it cool and not

let on we know. At least not yet."

Max hoped Sheriff Silva would follow through and ask Janice about Annie Worley. She and Pearla could not just come out with it. Better to build a relationship, maybe even a friendship, with Janice.

While in the sheriff's office, Max had noticed an old phone book being employed to balance a leg of Rene's desk and thought she remembered seeing some in the basement of the inn, the ideal source to find addresses of the older residents of Silvermist who may have known the elder Pete Worley. It occurred to Max how commonplace such an item was during her entire childhood and much of her young adult life. Phone directories and paper maps. She still preferred the tangible. Pen to paper, a leather-bound book or journal, a well-worn map which resisted being folded to its original form. Once technology had taken off, so much of life had changed.

"Yup, we have a bunch," Pearla confirmed. "I'll dig them out from the basement storage and we can look up some of the old timers. They'll be listed."

"Exactly what I was thinking. See, great minds think alike."

* * *

After locating his address and phone number in one of the old phone directories and fixing up another plate of snickerdoodle cookies, Max and Pearla drove to Mr. O'Leary's home. Max had tried the listed number, but it rang endlessly, with neither an answer nor a recorded message. Probably an old landline, which was still common in Silvermist. Even the inn had its original phone number and landline. If Mr. O'Leary wasn't home, they would leave a handwritten note on his door with a message to call the inn.

Just a few minutes drive from the Snowy Plover, the small home was tidy and well-kept from the outside. A sedan was parked in the driveway, so Max brightened at the thought they'd catch Mr. O'Leary at home. After a couple of knocks on the door, a garbled voice from within called out, "Be right there."

Mr. O'Leary came to the door in a frayed, striped button-up shirt that was missing all the buttons. It hung open, revealing an abundance of snow-white chest hair. Shorts and bare feet completed the look. Not that he was expecting visitors.

He held out his hand and greeted them warmly. The snickerdoodles sealed the invitation to come in. Mr. O'Leary led them through the small house to a screened-in porch.

"Now what can I do for you, ladies? I always appreciate a bit of company, though if I'd expected you, I would have been dressed nicer."

"No worries," Max reassured. "We're sorry to just pop in. I tried calling but I wasn't able to leave a message."

"I haven't figured out the whole message-box thing," Mr. O'Leary apologized. "That was always Helen's forte. And I haven't bothered with it since she passed. My friends know where to find me." He chuckled at this, then eyed Max and Pearla expectantly.

Pearla spoke up. "Actually, we came to see you because we're curious how you feel about the Worley property being sold."

A smile lit his face. "I've got great memories from the

golf course, I'll tell ya that. Beautiful little nine-holer. A whole group of us played there regularly while it lasted. We all thought it was a shame when it went under. After the fire at the clubhouse, it never recovered. Honestly, I've been hoping for years someone would restore it. I still like to play, but Brookhaven's getting to be too far a drive. I'll get out there again if the deal goes through."

"So, you'd be fine with a golf course?" Max asked. He nodded and reached for a cookie, then held out the plate to Max and Pearla. They politely declined.

"And what about the possibility of a housing tract with retail?" His eyes popped wide open at this suggestion.

"Absolutely not! Far as I know it's not zoned for that. No one who's lived here long would stand for it. Only an outsider would suggest it."

"We're concerned too, Mr. O'Leary. I just took ownership of the inn, and I'm not looking to change the makeup of Silvermist Point. There is nowhere else like it."

"That's right! Once this coastline is exploited, there's no going back. Silvermist is meant to be small." Worry lines formed deep creases across his forehead. "What have you heard?"

"Nothing official," Max paused, wanting to choose her words prudently. "Just that there are only two or three interested parties, so it would seem the sellers' options are limited if they want to unload the property quickly."

Pearla twirled a stray curl. "Do you know the family well? Maybe you could step in and speak with them about how detrimental it would be to the quiet life of Silvermist if a large residential development were to get approved for the site."

Good thinking, Pearla.

Mr. O'Leary ran his fingers through his sparse hair, then clenched his hands together before responding. "I knew Pete Senior, but I don't know his kids too well. Helen was the one to keep up with the neighbors' goings-on." He reached for another cookie. "Let's see, there's Pete Junior, the oldest, then Evan in the middle, and Seth. Pete Senior never would have wanted a housing tract or commercial development. He only agreed to the golf course because Seth used to play. He's probably rolling in his grave knowing the land is being sold. Pete Senior thought of it as his family legacy. I heard a rumor that Seth wants to sell it to a conservancy so it can't be developed at all."

"Oh, we heard that too." Max thought of the conversation she and Pearla overheard at Barnaby's.

"If the boys went that route, they could take a tax write-off and walk away. Then, no developers could touch it, and future generations could enjoy it. What do you ladies think?"

"I love that idea, but I'm okay with a small golf course too. Might be fun to learn the game. And a small course would bring visitors to Silvermist, but wouldn't overwhelm the town." Max couldn't think of a proper segue, so she came right out and asked, "Do you know anything about Annie Worley? You only mentioned the three brothers." Mr. O'Leary took another bite of his cookie before answering.

"Annie left Silvermist years ago. She said she wanted to find herself and wanted no part of the family's money. She didn't even show up for Pete's funeral. I thought that was really sad. Disrespectful even. Pete always doted on her, especially since his wife died."

No new information. After a few more minutes of polite chit-chat, Max and Pearla said goodbye and left Mr.

O'Leary's home with a promise to visit again, with more cookies.

Max took a detour past the Worley property rather than driving straight back to the inn. The main gate was closed, held together by a chain and padlock. No cars were parked inside. Next, she drove to one of the places where she knew the fence was breached. Someone had tried to secure this gate with a chain and lock, but someone else had made quick work of it with metal cutters.

"Shall we take another peek while no one's here?" Max asked.

"Why not?" Pearla was always up for anything.

"Should we park in the public lot again, or just leave the car here?" Max thought for a second before concluding that it was no big deal if they were seen on the property. They'd make up an excuse if needed, and after all, Char did say she was interested in buying. *I need to get a hold of her again to fill her in.*

"No, let's leave the car here and walk in. We won't stay long."

"I feel like we're sneaking around, trespassing," Pearla said, not hiding the glee from her voice.

"We are. But everyone does it. We'll make this quick," Max reasoned, justifying her actions.

They stayed under the cover of the trees along the fence-line, not wanting to be spotted out in the open of what must have once been a fairway, now overgrown with weeds as high as their waists. As they approached the front of the property, they heard voices, and could see three men from a distance. *I wonder where they got in?*

Pearla put her finger to her lips and shushed, then whispered, "Let's get closer and try to see who it is and

try to hear what they're saying." They crept closer to get a clearer vantage point.

"That's Jack Morehouse," Max whispered. "You can see his nose from a mile away."

Three men were talking animatedly with Jack Morehouse at the center of the group. He was directing two others to measure an area with a surveyor's tape. *What on earth is he doing here?* Pearla crouched low and crept closer as Max began to sweat. The only explanation was that Misty was reconsidering buying and sent Jack to survey the property. *But she would have told me, wouldn't she?*

A wave of dizziness overtook Max and she sat on the ground to let it pass. When Pearla turned, Max made an X sign with her hands, then motioned for her to come back. Pearla held up one finger to signal "Give me a minute," and she kept moving forward, crouching low behind thick foliage, while moving closer to the men. Jack stopped talking and looked straight in their direction.

Pearla went stock-still in a low crouch while Max stayed seated on the ground, holding her breath. She didn't know why she was gripped with fear, only that she was. Every part of her felt unsafe, but she couldn't understand why. She prayed the men wouldn't see them.

"You little turds better knock it off with the paintballing! We're not playing today. You're trespassing on private property!" Jack shouted in their direction.

Minutes seemed like hours until finally the small group of men moved further away and Pearla snuck back over to Max. Neither dared speak at first. Pearla took Max's hand and helped her up, leading the way back to the car. Not until they were in the car, seatbelts buckled and doors locked, did it feel safe to speak.

"That was beyond scary," Pearla said breathlessly.

"I know," Max agreed. "But why? We know Jack. He's been living at the inn for months. What were we so afraid of?"

"I don't trust him. He was rude to me at Barnaby's, but this was something more. I felt distinctly unsafe."

"Me too." Max rubbed her arms to chase away the goosebumps forming there.

"Since we know he's here, let's get back to the inn and search his room."

Max knew this was unethical and didn't need to tell Pearla that, but she was willing to do it under the guise of housekeeping.

"Sure, we can go back and tidy his room. It's probably due for a freshen-up."

"Right," Pearla winked. Max eased the car from the shoulder onto the road, then picked up speed.

"You grab the master key from the office and let's meet in your apartment." They could enter Jack's room from the interior hallway when the coast was clear. As they pulled into the parking lot, Max noticed that neither Misty's nor Jack's cars were there. The third interior upstairs room, a king suite, was not currently occupied by a guest, so they should be able to pull this off easily without having to explain themselves.

Max met Pearla in her apartment and peeked out the window to check the parking lot once again. They went through Pearla's door that connected with the upstairs hallway and snuck over to Jack's room, pausing at the closed door.

"It shouldn't feel as suspicious as it does," Pearla mused. Max knew it felt suspicious because it *was* suspicious.

Neither of them had cleaned the guest rooms since hiring part-time help. There was no good reason for them to enter.

"Here goes nothing," Pearla inserted the key into the lock and pushed the door open. Both women stepped inside quickly and closed it behind them. The main drapes were pulled open, but the sheers were drawn across the windows. The small space was disheveled, with a rumpled bed and a couple of towels thrown across a chair back. A golf bag stuffed with clubs was balanced against a wall.

"Oh my gosh, look!" Pearla was pointing at the top of an antique highboy dresser. On it sat what was unmistakably Misty's sheer turquoise scarf.

"We can't make assumptions," Max reminded Pearla. "Misty would've told us if she has something going on with Jack outside of their professional relationship." *At least I think so.*

"I'll check under the bed," Max said. She lifted the dust ruffle of the double bed and peered under, using her phone's flashlight. There was a medium-sized duffle bag. She pulled it out.

"Open it," Pearla encouraged. Only a second of hesitation, and Max pulled on the zipper. Both women gasped at what appeared to be a bulletproof vest in a camouflage pattern and a strange-looking gun.

"A paintball rifle?" Pearla said and took a couple of photos with her phone. Max zipped it back up and shoved it under the bed. She felt nervous and crunched for time. On the small wooden desk, sat a laptop with the charging cord plugged in. Pearla flipped it open.

"Password protected. Ugh!"

"Open the drawer," Max felt her pulse drumming in

her ears.

Pearla pulled the single drawer open and reached in. She unfurled a rolled-up paper revealing architectural renderings of the Worley property. The drawings showed what appeared to be streets and lot lines for homes. Many, many homes. Both women stood speechless as they took in the magnitude of the project.

"It goes all the way to the bluff," Max pointed. "This would never get approved to be built. There's no way. Also, why would Jack bother to have these plans drawn up when he hasn't made a bid on the property? It doesn't make sense."

Pearla considered that for a moment. "It doesn't have to, though. If he gets his hands on the land, he's going to push it through. He must have a plan in mind. Maybe the brothers are in on it?"

"That's possible, but what's with all the secrecy?" This was the part that Max couldn't work out. She paced the room to help her think. "Unless two of the brothers are going to sell it without the consent of the third? Maybe some sort of inside deal?"

"Then how do the other investors play into this?" Pearla continued to stare at the plans.

"They don't if they all drop out." Max sighed. "Or if they're murdered."

"That is really far-fetched," Pearla said, but her shaky voice betrayed her. "Besides, there's no way they can get away with that."

The sheer curtain fluttered as if it had caught an invisible breeze. *Amelia, you always have our backs.* Max stood on tiptoes and peeked out the window. Jack's truck was pulling into the lot.

"He's back. We need to get out." Pearla rolled the plans up, but not until she snapped a few photos on her phone. She opened the drawer and shoved the plans back in. Panic rose in Max's chest along with guilt for snooping. They slipped into the hall, then back inside Pearla's apartment. Pearla left the door cracked the tiniest bit, and they stood by, waiting.

Jack's voice drifted up the stairway. He had entered through the main lobby and taken the stairs from the living room.

"He's on his phone," Max said. They strained to decipher his words.

"Yes, I ran the numbers. If I can negotiate the price I want, I'll worry about the details later. I'm confident I can push it through." Max wished she could hear the other side of the conversation and know who was on the other end of the line. Just before Jack entered his room, he spoke again.

"With the right incentive, we'll sway them. The youngest one might need a bit more convincing though." Pearla closed her door. She and Max flopped onto the comfortable sofa to process what they'd heard.

Chapter 16

Wednesday
Pearla

After tossing and turning throughout the night, Pearla dragged herself out of bed, admitting defeat. The soft orange glow of the sun through her window convinced her; now was as good a time as any to get on with her day. She'd hoped a good night's sleep would provide a new perspective on the next course of action she and Max should take. Pearla was never one to sit quietly, keep her mouth closed, and wait to see what would unravel. She put the kettle on and set up the ceramic pour-over with her favorite dark roast coffee.

While waiting for the water to boil, she quickly dressed in black flared yoga pants and a comfortable t-shirt, then added an oversized sweatshirt, carefully pulling it over her head keeping her messy bun from falling apart. Her feet were toasty in floppy warm socks, as she never wore shoes inside. The coastal weather held a chill, even on an August morning. There was still time before she needed to set up the coffee and light breakfast spread downstairs, one of the many parts of her job that she loved.

Favorite red mug in hand, she folded herself onto her sofa, took a sip and sighed, then set the mug on the low table. She and Max had begun brainstorming and jotting down notes last night, and now she would look at them with fresh eyes. As fresh as she could be with little more than three hours' sleep. In addition to the notes, they'd made index cards with all of the suspects' names. Pearla placed the card with Jack Morehouse scrawled in sharpie, at the top. On separate cards were the names J.T. Fields, Nolan Briggs, Seth Worley, Evan Worley, Pete Worley Jr., Jason Martinez, Misty Caldwell, unknown paintballer, and one with a question mark.

"Really? We're counting Misty as a suspect?" Max had asked.

"Maybe not a suspect, but at least 'a person of interest.' Don't you think it's strange she knows nothing of Jack's plans? They're very close. Even closer than we thought, apparently, and he's her foreman after all." Then Pearla reassured Max by adding, "I'm certain once we speak with her, she'll clear things up."

Max had also questioned why the Worley brothers' names were written on the cards, reasoning, "Why would any of them want to sabotage their own deal? Makes no sense."

"Nothing's adding up yet. Max, you must trust the process. Let's talk about potential motives." Pearla loved a good mystery to solve, but didn't love being this close to it.

They agreed that the obvious motive was for one of the investors to eliminate the competition to improve his own chance of getting a good deal on the land, or just getting the land, period. Both had initially thought Jason Martinez was the likely murderer of Bruce Taylor, since Pearla had proven he had lied about his whereabouts at the time of the death. Unfortunately, he too, died under suspicious circumstances. They had to admit there was a low probability he'd killed Bruce, then accidentally died. So how were the two deaths connected? Were they connected?

Next, Pearla placed the cards of J.T. Fields and Nolan Briggs side by side underneath the card of Jack Morehouse. J.T. Fields had provided the weak alibi that he'd been walking the beach at the time of Bruce Taylor's death, and Nolan Briggs had not arrived in Silvermist until the next day. *Maybe I can get Rene to question Nolan regarding his whereabouts on Sunday.*

She looked at the cards with the three Worley brothers' names and placed them underneath the cards of Nolan Briggs and J.T. Fields. Pete Junior and Evan were eyewitnesses to Bruce Taylor's death, so they could not be suspects, unless they hired someone to do it. No, that was a stretch and still didn't address the *why*. Pearla was thinking out loud, as she often did when she was alone. The youngest brother, Seth, was not present at the time Bruce was hit. Pearla moved his card up a row.

Time to consider the second possible murder. Unfortunately, there was not an exact time for Jason Martinez's death, only an approximation. He'd borrowed a bike from the inn and had intended to be at the property to meet with the Worleys, but never showed up. By the time his body was discovered in the ditch, the meeting was well underway. Was it possible Jason was targeted by someone at that meeting? They would have had to run him off the road sometime before the meeting began.

Pearla's attention was drawn back to Jack. Where had Jack been at the time of Bruce Taylor's death, and who could corroborate it? Shortly after Jason Martinez's body was discovered, Pearla had run into Jack in the parking lot at Barnaby's, and he'd been acting strangely—rude and out of character. Was it because he'd run Jason off the road just a short while earlier? *Whoa!* Pearla took another long gulp of coffee and savored the taste, then stood up to stretch her legs.

She stepped over to the window and gazed out. Jack's car was still in the lot where he'd parked it last night. She noticed the glow of lights on at Max's. *Bet she didn't sleep either.* Pearla found her phone and sent Max a text. Max responded right away, saying to come over. Pearla pulled on her sheepskin boots, which were sitting by the door connecting her apartment to the interior hall.

She closed the door softly and looked across the hall, which was lit with dim, low-wattage lights as required. Pearla wondered if Jack was awake. Usually if one of the guests was in the hall restroom, you could tell from the light shining through the obscured glass panel in the door. It was dark. This was the bathroom currently shared by the two rooms Jack and Misty were occupying during the construction period of the Getaway Ranch and Spa. All was quiet. Pearla went down the stairs, through the lobby, and out the front door. It was a short walk to Max's stone cottage. She knocked three times, then used her key to enter.

Max was seated on the bench at the dining table. She looked up and removed her reading glasses when Pearla entered. Copies of the *Silvermist Point of View* newsletters were spread before her.

"I've been up for hours," Max confessed. "Char sent a message in the middle of the night. I called her back and filled her in with what's going on. After that, I had trouble going back to sleep, so I dug into these. I'm arranging them by year. I found the one announcing Pete Senior's death and the notice for his memorial service. His sons wrote a touching tribute and obituary."

Pearla held out her hand. "Can I see that issue?" She scanned through it, then looked at the next issue. This one spoke of the lovely service and the songs played and included another tribute to Pete Worley Senior.

"There's a photo of a floral wreath here with the caption, 'Beautiful flowers sent by Annie Worley, Pete's beloved daughter, who wasn't able to attend in person, but sent her condolences.' Interesting. These versions of the newsletter are less … what's the word?"

"Gossipy? Rude? Inflammatory?" Max raised her eyebrows.

"Yes, they're actually just news reports and articles about events happening in town. I wonder when the tone changed." Pearla picked up a few more back issues. The last issue distributed before the current one was from six months ago, with the headline proclaiming "Suspicious Injury at the Snowy Plover Inn." As she read through the recent issue again, something struck her. She waved the copy toward Max before reading.

"Max, it says, and I quote, 'Rumors of the property being cursed have resurfaced.' What does that mean? Who said the property is cursed?"

"I'm not sure how we glossed over that before. I'll see if Janice is free for lunch and maybe a little wine tasting at Gracious Grapes today. Maybe I can get her to talk. I doubt she'll straight out admit she's the author of the SMPOV, but I'm betting some wine might get her to open up."

"Good thinking," Pearla agreed. "So did Char have any thoughts about what's happening in Silvermist?" Pearla felt like there were answers hovering around her; it was only a matter of asking the right questions of the right people to make sense of the situation. She looked expectantly at Max.

"Char's as surprised as we are about Jack; she offered to look into his background and dig around a little."

Pearla nodded her head, remembering how Char had dug into a previous guest's online presence. Since inheriting her fortune, Char had learned to sharpen this skill to protect herself from those who might try to take advantage of her. "Great idea. Do you think she'll be able to get a decent Wi-Fi signal?"

"Yes, when she's at the resorts, just not during the safaris. She's not exactly roughing it."

Pearla could picture Char looking beautiful and perfect while everyone else was sweaty and dusty.

"She said she's been feeling really good, too. Her arthritis hasn't flared up at all."

Pearla knew Char followed a strict regimen to keep her autoimmune disease in check. Thankfully, she had attentive doctors and with the right diet, exercise, and cocktail of medications, she was able to participate in all sorts of adventures.

"As soon as she finds anything worth noting, she'll

send us a file. So, we should be checking our email for it. I turned on my alerts."

"Alright, I'll go get the order from Front Porch, then set up the breakfast spread. I'll hang around in the living room. If an opportunity to speak with Jack or the investors presents itself, I'll take it. Misty too, for that matter. You arrange to meet with Janice, and I'll join you if I can."

"Sounds like a plan," Max agreed.

* * *

Pearla parallel parked in front of the bakery. There were already a couple of early-bird customers rocking in the colorful wooden chairs and sipping their drinks on the front porch. The inviting scent of strong coffee mingled with cinnamon and baked goods wafted out the door, and Pearla inhaled deeply. She entered to find her order, neatly boxed in one of the signature pink containers. As an afterthought, she asked the barista for two cinnamon rolls, knowing Max would appreciate her favorite indulgence.

The girl behind the counter scooped vanilla icing from a vat warming on the stove and ladled it onto each cinnamon roll, only adding to the catastrophic calorie count. Worth it.

Pearla sighed appreciatively, then snapped a photo and sent it to Max with the message: Couldn't resist.

She checked her phone and decided there was no time to enjoy a coffee on the porch. As she headed out, balancing the two boxes and pushing the glass door, she nearly bumped into Tyne, who was on his way in.

"Hey," he said, then whispered, "I've got some information for you and Max. Mind if I stop by the inn?"

"Of course not," Pearla responded, her mind buzzing

with possibilities. "I'll see you there, gotta get back." As soon as she got into her car, Pearla's phone pinged. A text from Max read: Char found out Jack's uncle owns a massive development company. She sent the details to us. *Interesting.*

* * *

Setting up the living room for guests was becoming muscle memory for Pearla, and something she enjoyed. Coffee, tea, and hot chocolate were available along with a tray of pastries and some fresh whole fruit. The spread was out from seven-thirty to nine-thirty and then cleared away with a note directing guests to the kitchen if they missed the window. There they could use the single cup coffee maker or tea kettle, find milk or cream in the fridge, and grab a leftover pastry or other snack or fruit left thoughtfully on the sideboard.

She and Max decided it didn't cost too much to provide this light breakfast, and guest feedback indicated it was very appreciated. Though they'd thought about closing off access to the kitchen from guests, they hadn't. Besides, there was no practical way to secure the two swinging doors connecting the reception and living room to the kitchen. However, both the entrance to the cellar and the basement were secured with locks after the unfortunate incident involving a guest during the grand re-opening of the inn.

The tantalizing smell of brewed coffee soon filled the living room, and Pearla poured herself another cup, while reminding herself she'd need to drink water for the rest of the day. She set her mug down on the reception counter in the foyer and spread out the newspaper which was still delivered daily to the inn, left in a cubby under the rural mailbox out on Snowy Plover Lane.

Minutes later, she was joined by Max, who took her place on the stool next to Pearla. With the double pocket sliding doors fully open, they were in a position to see who came and went from the living room.

Pearla had set a plate, napkin, and fork out for Max. Her cinnamon roll was still in the pink box. Pearla was halfway through hers and enjoying every bite.

"I almost suggested we split one, but nope. I will be eating this entire delightful treat." Pearla shoved in a bite.

"Good call," Max agreed. "If you're gonna indulge, you must eat it all." And she dug in, unraveling the outer layer.

First to arrive for breakfast were the teenage boys. Pearla was surprised they were up. Both wore flannel pajama pants, t-shirts, and slides. Their mussed-up hair and loping walk reminded Pearla of the boys from her former job at Royal High School who wore pajama pants to school on a regular basis. She glanced at Max and read her friend's thoughts.

"He'll be here in a couple of weeks," Pearla reassured.

Max smiled through teary eyes. "How did you know I was missing Sawyer?"

"Just did."

They chewed thoughtfully while watching the lanky boys as they made themselves hot chocolates and piled on the whipped cream. Next, they grabbed bananas and pastries and headed out the French doors and up the stairs to the tower.

"I hope they don't get crumbs on the window cushions. When we're ready to replace those, we should do waterproof, stain-proof fabric," Pearla thought aloud.

Max tapped her with a foot. Jack was walking down the stairs from his room. They waved and said hello in unison, and Jack grunted back a barely intelligible response while holding up his hand in a stiff wave.

"See? Rude. Like the other day," Pearla whispered. Max jumped down from her stool, followed Jack, and cornered him in the living room near the coffee condiments. Pearla watched in fascination.

"How are you, Jack? I feel like I haven't seen much of you lately. Been busy at the Getaway?"

"Yes. Very busy. Long days and late nights, but it's coming together."

"So, I was wondering. When you finish up construction at the Getaway, what are your plans? I heard your uncle's company has projects all over the world. Big and small."

Jack added cream to his coffee and paused mid-pour, setting the pitcher down roughly. He placed his hands on his hips and faced Max. Pearla hoped she was dead wrong, but his stance looked aggressive. She crossed the distance and joined them in time to hear Jack say, "Excuse me, but what do you know of my uncle's development company?"

"Only what I've just said." Max stood waiting for his response while Jack turned to gather a plate, tension thick in the air, as at least a minute passed with no reply.

"Not to butt in, Jack," Pearla added, "but you seem really tense. Is everything okay?"

A scowl of pure annoyance crossed his face before he responded, unable to hide his sarcasm. "That's kind of you to ask. I'm fabulous. As I said, I'm busy with work, and I prefer to keep my personal life personal, if you don't mind."

Alrighty then.

"Sure, no problem," Pearla said as she and Max watched him walk out to the patio area of the courtyard, obviously wanting to end the conversation.

"Shoot," Max said. "I shouldn't have said that about his uncle's company. Now he'll just avoid us even more."

They reclaimed their spots behind the reception counter and resumed eating their cinnamon rolls. A few minutes later, Chief came bursting through the propped-open front door, prancing excitedly. Tyne followed shortly after.

"Whoops, I meant to tell you he was stopping by," Pearla said as they watched him wrangle Chief and clip on his leash.

"Sorry, we're still working on manners. I thought he'd be tired from the walk over, but this guy has boundless energy."

"He's welcome here anytime," Max said. "How is he around cats?"

"My parents' ancient cat has put him in his place, so he has a healthy respect for felines." Tyne addressed Chief. "Don'tcha boy? You know who's boss."

"Good," Max smiled. "Maybe he'll meet Butters and they can be friends."

Pearla grabbed a can of treats from the kitchen and shook them, calling for Butters out the front door. In no time, a streak of beige fur shot through the door at the sound of his treats, and stopped abruptly as soon as he spotted Chief. The fur along the cat's spine rose up and he aimed a low growl at the intruder.

Chief took a few wary steps closer while Tyne held the leash. The dog put his snout to the ground, then lay flat, and finally flipped onto his back in full surrender mode.

This display satisfied Butters, who appeared to accept the gesture of submission from Chief. He skulked over and rubbed against the dog, then flopped down next to him as Max and Pearla melted at the cuteness. Both boys received treats.

After offering Tyne a snack from the living room, they gathered in the office, wanting privacy. Chief trotted in with them and began sniffing. Tyne explained why he had come over to speak with them.

"Seems everyone was at the bar last night. And everyone was drinking," he began. "All three of the Worley brothers, both of the investors too. Janice showed up. Even Sheriff Silva stopped in after his shift, plus a bunch of others from town. Misty, Jack … it was packed. Honestly, unusual for a Tuesday night."

"Huh, so Jack went back out last night…" Pearla interrupted, thinking aloud. "Sorry, go on."

"I overheard snippets of conversations, but the name Annie Worley kept popping up." Now Tyne really had their attention. "Apparently, she contacted her brothers after years of silence."

"Why?" Max asked. "Any information about why?"

"Well, after I heard Annie had contacted her brothers, Janice came in by herself and sat at the bar. She always knows everybody's business, so I asked her what she thought about Annie contacting her family after so much time away. According to Janice, Seth is the one who reached out to Annie, and she finally responded. Seth told Annie about the sale, and according to him, she doesn't think the family land should be developed."

"We don't think Seth wants that either," Max interjected.

"Right, but word is the other brothers are planning to

force the sale, regardless. And I think they could have. It was two against one. Annie was assumed to be completely out of the picture until she supposedly sent a group text to her brothers. Honestly, it seems fishy to me. Some of the people who knew her even suggested she might not be alive." Tyne looked from one to the other.

"What if the texts are fake and not actually from her?" Max said, and Pearla nodded in agreement.

"That's what the two older brothers think. But Janice admitted she gets mail for Annie at the post office and is responsible for forwarding it. Janice does not believe Annie is dead." Chief kept sniffing at the bags on the floor in the corner. Tyne reached out to grab the dog's collar. "Sit, boy. What are you so interested in?"

"Those are the belongings of the two dead guys," Pearla said. "If only dogs could talk. I'd ask him what he's thinking."

"Is the sheriff coming to pick those up?" Tyne asked, as Pearla realized they hadn't yet told Rene about the helpful thing they'd done. Max changed the subject before Pearla had to explain.

"Do you think Annie'll show up in person?"

"That's what the brothers are demanding because no one has seen her in years, and no one knows how to find her."

"Wow, Tyne. I wonder if Annie will actually show up. This is an interesting plot twist. Super far-fetched, but do you think she's behind the deaths in some way?" Pearla felt she had to ask.

"I was wondering the same," Max said in support.

"I'd be lying if I told you I didn't consider it."

"The fact that she's off the grid and doesn't care

about money tracks with her objecting to the land being developed. Maybe she feels compelled to speak up against it," Pearla said. "If it's really her sending texts."

Max and Pearla both thanked Tyne for sharing the new information, and in an afterthought, Pearla asked if he'd speak with Colby about paintballing.

"We know Colby plays. We saw his equipment at the house when we cleared Beth's belongings to help Larry. Neither of us has come up with a plausible reason to ask him about it, though. But if you acted curious about it, he'd probably talk."

Tyne couldn't disguise the huge grin that spread across his face. "So, you're letting me into your investigation is what I'm hearing, ladies. I'm happy to help. I'll get Colby to talk, and I'll report back."

With Max planning to take Janice to Gracious Grapes, Tyne pumping Colby for information, and herself on alert at the inn, Pearla was confident they'd find some answers.

Chapter 17

Max

Rather than wait for Janice to call her, Max called the Post Stop directly, hoping she would answer. After three rings, Janice picked up.

"Silvermist Post Stop, may I help you?"

Max was pleased, but then needed to think quickly. She'd neglected to plan what to say. A quick hello followed by an invitation. She crossed her fingers Janice would accept, as the words spilled forth in a rush.

"Hi, Janice. It's Max, Maxine, from the inn." *Ugh, stop babbling. She knows who you are.* "Are you free to meet at Gracious Grapes today by any chance? I'm stopping in to see Marjory about some of the new wines and canapés. She's got a whole fall theme planned for the tasting room, and I've offered to sample it."

No pause at all. "Why, Maxine. That sounds like a lot of fun. What time did you have in mind?"

"I need to meet with Sheriff Silva first, then we can walk over after, if that works. Like two-fifteen?" Max knew Janice would savor that tidbit.

"Yes, I'll see you then."

The part about visiting Sheriff Silva was truly inspired.

As luck would have it, Sheriff Silva was available and Max arrived at his office just before two. The tension in her shoulders relaxed when she realized Janice was not standing guard at her usual spot behind the counter of the post office, enjoying a full view of whomever came and went. Max darted past and opened the door to the sheriff's office. As she stepped into the cramped space, she once again closed the door behind her for privacy. Max got straight to business and asked Sheriff Silva if he knew Annie had contacted her brothers and if he'd looked into it.

"You know I can't comment on an ongoing investigation."

Not this again.

"C'mon Rene. We're past that, and you've already decided both deaths were not accidental. Plus, what does Annie Worley have to do with any of that?"

"What do you think she has to do with it?" he countered, leaning forward on his elbows.

Chapter 18

Pearla

Pearla stacked the mugs and plates in the dishwasher. She rinsed the metal filter and plunger from the twenty-cup coffee machine, and set them on a tea towel to dry. She covered the tray of leftover pastries in plastic film and left it out on the long counter. Then she nestled the remaining fruit in a smaller decorative bowl. All the while, she replayed and tried to process the conversation she'd overheard between Nolan Briggs and J.T. Fields.

She had been surprised to see them sharing one of the small round tables in the living room, and had surreptitiously begun to straighten the books on the shelves nearest them. She fiddled with her phone and put in her earbuds. If they paid her any attention, they'd think she was listening to music, not their conversation.

"Now that we're the only two investors left, we should leverage it to our advantage. Neither of us has put in a formal offer, but I'm sure you have a figure in mind, same as I do," Briggs said.

"How do I know you aren't behind the 'removal', shall we say, of the competition?" Fields said.

These two are so arrogant, they don't even attempt to lower their voices.

"Oh, please, do I look like a killer to you? I've never met those unfortunate men in my life. Besides, I could ask the same of you. How do I know you're not plotting my demise to clear the path for yourself?"

Fields laughed at the suggestion before responding. "Well, I'm not. I suppose you'll have to trust me on that."

"You'll have to trust me as well," Briggs said.

Fields tapped his fingers on the table, appearing to mull the suggestion over before asking, "So what're you thinking?"

Briggs actually raised his voice even more in his apparent excitement. Pearla did not have to make much of an effort to hear every word.

"We team up and lowball the owners. Then we develop the property together or resell it and split the profit. You'd be a total fool not to consider it. The brothers don't have a clue what they're doing. I happen to know they have an enormous overdue tax bill, and none of them has the capital to pay it, or to buy out their siblings. If you and I play this right, we could profit big time."

Fields didn't respond immediately, and Pearla was reluctant to move out of earshot. She watched Briggs scribble something on a napkin and slide it over to Fields. It felt like a scene from a movie.

"This is the figure I have in mind." Pearla watched Fields pick up the napkin and nod slowly, saying, "I'm in. Set up a meeting."

"Let's shake on it," Briggs requested. "I don't want to look too eager. We need to make 'em sweat a little. We're gonna make 'em think we're both backing out."

"Sounds good," Fields said and stood up.

"One more thing." Briggs' voice seemed to deepen and change into something sinister. "Don't dare double-cross me. Or you'll regret it."

"Same goes for you," Fields replied, but in a voice more meek than sinister.

It was a lot to think about, and as Pearla replayed the conversation again, she wondered what about this specific property had people so stirred up? She knew greed was a motivating factor in good people making bad choices and committing crimes. *They didn't call it the green-eyed monster for nothing. Or was that jealousy, greed's best friend?* Her thoughts were abruptly interrupted by the ringing of the old rotary phone on the reception desk. She hustled from the kitchen to answer it.

"Hello, you've reached the Snowy Plover Inn."

"Who is this, please?" The female voice on the other end held an edge of stress.

"My name is Pearla Beckett. How can I help you today?"

"Oh. I'd like to speak with Mable Evans."

"I'm sorry, Mable and Kevin have retired, but I'm the new manager and I'll be happy to help with anything you need. A reservation, perhaps?"

"Um, okay, I suppose. I need to book a room for a week, maybe longer. Do you have any available?"

"What dates are you thinking of?" Pearla pulled the date book from the drawer. She would add the reservation to the digital calendar later. So far, she and Max had kept the traditional date book. It was convenient to have the reservations recorded in two places.

"I'd like to arrive tomorrow."

"We can make that work."

Before Pearla could say which options were available, the woman spoke again, her words pouring out in a rush. "My name's Ann." She paused. "Hannah. My name's Hannah. Hannah Smith. Is it okay if I pay in cash, please? I don't use credit cards. I know Mable would have let me. She knew me well."

"Cash is fine," Pearla reassured. "We'll have a room all ready for you. The master suite is available, or one of our standard queen rooms. All of them are quite comfortable. The suite is priced higher, though."

"I want the suite; I don't care about the cost. I can afford it," Hannah said defensively.

"I didn't mean to imply you couldn't." *Sheesh, I'm only trying to inform you.*

"I'll arrive tomorrow afternoon."

"Great, we'll be expecting you." Pearla tried to exude kindness through the phone.

"I have one more request."

"Sure, how can I help?" Pearla asked.

"If I don't show up, please call me to, um, remind me. I'll give you my cell number." The woman rattled off her number. Then the conversation took a strange turn.

"If I don't respond, I'm going to give you a second number to call, but only call it if I don't show up by the evening, or don't respond to your reminder. If you call the second number, you're to let the person who answers know I'm booked at the inn." *What is this lady getting at?* Pearla was about to respond when the woman spoke again.

"Please, just say you will. There's a good tip if you just promise and don't ask questions."

"Sure thing. That's no problem at all. We look forward to having you as our guest. See you tomorrow afternoon."

"Right. Goodbye." The call disconnected.

Pearla paused to consider the odd conversation.

Chapter 19

Maxine

When Max exited Sheriff Silva's office, she found Janice at the counter of the post office wearing a nonchalant expression that looked painted on.

"You ready, Janice? It's lovely out." Max kept her voice casual.

"Sure, let me just grab my purse, and put up my counter sign." Janice moved the hands on a wooden clock to indicate she'd be back at four, just an hour before closing. Too bad for anyone who had a package to send. Max had already learned the Post Stop was not to be counted upon to be open during its regular business hours. Janice fumbled behind the counter, then held up her giant purse victoriously. *Good, she's not going to remark about my talking to the sheriff.*

"So, what were you visiting Sheriff Silva for? If you don't mind my asking."

"I had a question about a regulation regarding the inn. Just boring stuff. I was hoping he could point me in the right direction, to the proper resource." *Nice one.*

"Oh," Janice said with obvious disappointment.

Gracious Grapes was located on the other side of the park, in the middle of the village square. They could walk straight through the green space or take the path around the square and pass some of the other businesses of Silvermist along the way. Max assumed Janice would not appreciate trekking through grass, so she started on the sidewalk, taking the longer route, and hoping Janice would talk about the village businesses.

"How long have these storefronts been vacant?" Max asked.

Janice jumped a little at the question, as if she'd been momentarily lost in thought. "Some only appear vacant. I happen to know residents who use the space for an office, but they don't have a sign. So, it looks empty when it's not. Like this one." Janice pointed at a little building with no sign. "Most of the open businesses you see have been here for ages." She began to list them off.

"There's Books and Brew— decent, but overpriced coffee, if you ask me, but a fair selection of books. Front Porch Bakery, best baked goods— you can't beat them. Let's see, Miscellaneous Goods—every kind of fancy artisan food and drinks. It's too expensive for everyday shopping. I go into Brookhaven myself and stock up at the Super Mart, much less pricey. There's only two real restaurants, as you know— Mama's Pizza and Barnaby's.

Both are excellent. I patronize them often."

Max couldn't get a word in edge-wise, but, no matter. Janice's talking and rambling was exactly what she wanted.

"Have you been inside Everything, Everything Emporium?" Janice pointed at the hunter green awning. "I'm not sure how that place survives. It's so similar to Surroundings. Plus, I'm not into buying used things." Janice turned up her nose and sniffed. "You never know who owned that stuff before."

Max had visited E.E. Emporium and Surroundings and found them to be distinct from each other, both with eclectic items one could not buy just anywhere. Surroundings offered a variety of home goods and furnishings, while Everything, Everything had a bit of *everything*—clothes, dishes, used books, jewelry, you name it.

"Hmm, I disagree. I think the stores complement each other. Some small towns have loads of second-hand and vintage stores all next to each other. People love treasure hunting, you know." Janice nodded in distracted acknowledgment.

Max remembered that she and Pearla had promised Larry they would go through Beth's jewelry and have it appraised. She brought her focus back to Janice's ongoing commentary of the village businesses.

"Now, the newest businesses are the real estate office, the yoga studio, the law office, and Gracious Grapes. I can't say for certain how they are all doing financially, but I believe Gracious Grapes does well. I always see people going in and out with bags and boxes. And the wine isn't cheap."

"You know a lot about the village, Janice. I'm impressed." *Maybe a little flattery will help.*

"Well, I've been working at the Mail Stop for ages. Nothing gets past me," Janice boasted. Max thought this was a perfect opening to ask about the *Silvermist Point of View* and its authorship, but they were in front of Gracious Grapes, so she pushed the door open and led the way in.

"Let's first say hi to Marjory, then we can decide where to sit," Max suggested.

The large, open room had a long counter with all the wine varieties on display behind it. Customers choosing to do a tasting picked three reds and three whites, or two reds, two whites and two blush wines from a list on the chalkboard. Marjory was known to pour generously during tastings. Knowing this, Max suggested they each taste a flight of wines and split a platter of Marjory's new fall preview snack combination. Janice voiced her enthusiastic approval and agreed to let Marjory select the wines for them.

They chose a tall, two-person table with high-backed swivel stools near the counter, where they could converse with Marjory, and tasted their first wine. The sampler tray had samosas, green olives, garlic croutons, tart apple slices, cheese wedges, pumpkin puff pastries, and focaccia with flavored oil for dipping. It was a delicious blend of sweet and savory. Max hoped the wine would loosen Janice's tongue and encourage her to speak freely. Marjory was quick to pour glass two as soon as Janice finished her first.

After some light banter about Max's previous career as an English teacher and Janice's brief stint as a journalist for the Brookhaven newspaper, which Max made a mental note to revisit, Max went for it with a more substantial question.

"Janice, I was wondering how well you knew Annie

Worley before she left town. Do the two of you talk much these days?"

Janice paused before answering, as if she was constructing her response carefully. "It's been over seven years since she left. We never knew each other well; she's obviously far younger than me. I knew Pete Senior, though." Janice leaned in and lowered her voice to a whisper, though no one was there to hear her other than Marjory.

"Nobody knows this, but Pete and I had just started seeing each other, if you know what I mean. It was shortly before he passed away. He'd finally gotten over, well, you never really get over, I suppose, his wife's death…" she trailed off.

"You and Mr. Worley were dating?" Max hoped her tone would not betray her surprise. She focused on keeping her expression neutral.

"Well, I don't think you could call it dating. We were just getting to the stage where we might have dated. Sadly, we never got the chance."

"I'm sorry to hear that, Janice." Max waved over Marjory who came quickly, and generously poured a third tasting for both women. It was more like an almost-full glass.

"We hadn't spoken in days and I thought it was his way of playing hard-to-get. You know, not returning my calls and such. I was waiting and hoping for him to make the next move and come into the Mail Stop or call me, and then I heard the horrible news." She stopped to take a hefty sip of her wine, then let out a small hiccup and said, "Oh, excuse me."

"So, Annie had already left town when her father died?" Max asked.

"Yes, I'm not certain how she found out. Her brothers must have contacted her, but she didn't come back to Silvermist for the funeral. She sent a beautiful floral wreath though."

"When did Annie set up a post box for herself? Was it right before she left town?" Max hoped Janice was tipsy enough not to wonder why she was asking such specific questions.

"No, no, Annie had a post box for a while. After she left Silvermist, she kept it and sent a money order once a year to renew it."

"Then who picked up her mail if she wasn't in town?"

Max thought she might be pushing her luck, and doubted Janice would answer. It was probably a violation of privacy and certainly not her business. However, Janice did answer, sort of. She told Max no one physically picked up the mail. A couple times a year, a package was sent with directions to empty the box and send all the contents in the package to the specified address. According to Janice, she complied and sent the package on. Max burned to know where the package was sent, but knew better than to push it.

Instead, Max brought the line of questioning, disguised as innocent conversation, back to the present, asking, "Do you think it's actually Annie who contacted her brothers? Because I think it might be someone posing as her. I mean how do we know she's really still alive?"

Janice gasped and almost choked on a bite of focaccia, as she exclaimed, "Maxine! Why would you say that? Annie's not dead. I just told you she has an active post box at the Mail Stop."

"Yes, you did tell me that, but from what you've said,

doesn't it at least seem plausible that someone else is keeping it, not Annie? You haven't actually spoken with her."

"I don't know where you get your crazy ideas." Janice's tone betrayed her and Max sensed she was considering there was room for speculation.

Glass number four of wine was going down smoothly. Max had signaled Marjory to stop at just a sip for her, but Marjory generously filled Janice's glass to over half, encouraging her to identify the notes of raspberry, and telling her how glad she was that Janice had finally found the time to stop in for a tasting.

"I'd have come sooner, but I don't have many friends these days." Janice took another sip and her eyes watered. Max reached over, resting her hand on Janice's arm.

"I'm sorry. I know you and Beth were close friends. It's hard to lose someone you love. I never had the chance to know Beth, but I feel like I know her a little since I helped Larry sort through her belongings. She was a talented woman." Janice raised her eyebrows, and set down her glass.

"Talented? How do you mean?"

"Well, the newspaper, the SMPOV," Max explained innocently.

"You don't think she wrote it do you?" Janice snorted, then put her hand to her nose.

"Janice, I know she wrote it. Beth had every single copy for the last twenty-five years. Why else would anyone keep every copy?"

"Max, trust me. Beth was not the author of the SMPOV. I was her best friend, and I'm telling you, she did not write it. Besides, lots of people collect stuff."

"Ok, then who wrote it? And who took up the torch? Did you notice the paper ceased after Beth's death and only appeared again this week after going silent for six months?" Max kept her tone neutral, but found her frustration level mounting. She'd presented Janice with irrefutable evidence, and Janice had flat out denied that Beth wrote it. Now what? Janice chewed thoughtfully before responding.

"I haven't a clue who wrote it then or now." Janice popped an olive into her mouth.

Max leaned on an elbow and frowned before conceding. "Alright. I truly thought it was Beth. I guess I was wrong."

As much as Max yearned to suggest that Janice had now taken over for Beth, or that they'd worked together all along, she held her tongue. Apparently, Janice was not going to budge. *Maybe she really doesn't know who the author is.* Marjory came over with a tray of sweets, then poured the fifth wine sample.

"Just a sip," Max requested, thinking she still had things to do that did not include an afternoon nap.

"A little more, please." Janice held out her glass. "I'll hardly get the flavor with that bitty amount."

Marjory tipped the bottle, adding to Janice's glass, then pulled over a third tall stool and sat down to join them. She asked what they thought about the fall snack choices. Max loved them all. Janice said they were 'different,' but good, except the focaccia bread was too dry.

"There was something else I wanted to ask you, Janice." Max figured she may as well take a chance. "In the last issue of the newsletter it mentioned the Worley property being cursed, or rumored to be cursed. Do you know anything about that?"

"I noticed that too," Marjory said in support.

Max watched Janice's expression carefully. If Janice was hiding something, she gave nothing away. She sniffed and rolled her eyes, then took another swig of wine before answering.

"Maxine, that's an old joke. Nothing but a rumor. Kids have always snuck in on dares and messed around. That property has always been left wild, other than the brief time it had the nine-hole golf course. Some people believe the curse caused the clubhouse to burn, but the authorities said it was faulty wiring."

"There must have been an article about it in the SMPOV. I'll try to look it up in the archives," Max said.

"Oh, I'm sure there's an article, but it can't give you the complete details like I can," Janice said, smirking.

"Do tell," Max said, raising her eyebrows.

"Well, I shouldn't gossip," Janice hedged and took a sip of wine. "But it was a long time ago, so there's no harm."

OMG, get on with it, Janice.

"Pete Worley Senior originally developed that golf course with Seth in mind; he's the baby of the family. However, Seth wasn't interested in it. He'd given up golf and was on to something else. So, Pete and his wife offered it to the other brothers to manage when Pete was ready to retire. Pete Junior and Evan were considering it. But before they could decide, it mysteriously burned down. A lot of people thought Seth was behind it, out of spite. He didn't want it, but he didn't want his brothers to get it either."

"Do you think it's true? Do you think Seth burned it down on purpose?" Max asked.

"I did at the time," Janice said. "They never rebuilt, obviously. Now I understand it's used for some type of illegal gun sport. Guns that shoot paint or some such.

Hopefully, the new owner will put a stop to it."

"You're in favor of the sale then? Would you want to see it developed with housing or another golf course? All the talk I've been hearing is focused on concerns about over-development. A golf course, residents are okay with, but a big development or housing units is most definitely not popular with the locals," Marjory said.

Max was grateful Marjory had been the one to ask, fearing Janice's patience with her questions might wear thin.

Janice's answer surprised her. "I don't have an opinion one way or the other. It doesn't matter to me. I'm old, and I could retire if I wanted to. I guess I'd prefer Silvermist never change at all, but it's inevitable. Don't you think the spa is going to increase traffic here? Change is coming whether we like it or not, ladies." She downed the last of glass number five.

"Let's have that last taste." Janice held up her glass with a shaky hand.

"You go ahead." Max passed on the last pour, she wanted her wits sharp.

Janice finished her last taste quickly. Max settled the bill, saying it was her treat. They said goodbye to Marjory and left. Janice suggested they take the shorter route through the park, and Max watched her closely, not wanting to have her take a tumble on the uneven grass. Janice stopped under the giant, ancient oak tree, hands on her hips, and gazed up into the branches.

"Isn't it magnificent? Have you ever stood here and truly admired the beauty of this tree, Maxine? People don't often appreciate the things right in front of them."

"Janice, I love this tree. It's one of the things solidified in my childhood memories of Silvermist." Max gave Janice the short version of her past relationship with the town and what had drawn her back, as they stood in the broad afternoon shade of the oak.

"I'm pleased to know you appreciate it properly," Janice said. "This tree has a rich history. It stood here long before we were born and will remain as a sentinel of the town long after we pass away." She walked around the massive trunk. Higher up the tree, the trunk split in two.

"There's a knothole where the suitor of Amelia, she's your ghost, you know, left notes for her. It's still here. I can show you if you like."

That unlocked a memory in Max. She and Char had first learned the story of Amelia in their childhood days as visitors to the inn.

"I was told Amelia's suitor left the notes in an exposed root," Max said thoughtfully.

Janice pointed out the knothole, which looked like a perfect hidey hole and said, "Well, it's an old story, another old rumor. There are probably lots of versions of it. This town has many tales that are passed down. You'll see the longer you live here."

"It's my home now," Max said. "I never plan to leave."

"Me neither," Janice agreed.

Max took her phone from her purse, wanting to give a subtle signal that she needed to get on with her day. "Janice, we'll have to get together again soon. Thanks for joining me. I've got to hurry back to work." Max noticed she had several texts and missed messages.

Chapter 20

Pearla

Should we wait for Max to get back or do you want me to tell you what I found out?" Tyne asked when Pearla returned his call. Pearla was dying to hear what he had to say, but figured they should wait for Max so she wouldn't have to relay the information secondhand.

"Send her a text and see if she can come to the bar. I'll send her one too and say it's urgent." Neither got a response back.

Ninety minutes later, Max called Pearla, apologizing for the missed calls, and breathlessly asking what was so important.

"Tyne has news. He spoke with Colby and the middle Worley brother."

Max had news of her own. "Besides the texts and calls from you and Tyne, Pete Worley tried to call me three times while I was at Gracious Grapes with Janice. I had notifications off, so I never heard it. Should I call him right now, or wait so you can listen in?"

"Did he leave a message?"

"A short one asking me to call him back as soon as possible. No details."

"Call him now, then call me right back. No, actually, just meet me at Barnaby's after you call him." Pearla chewed on a nail before she realized what she was doing. That had been a hard habit to break, and she didn't want to start it up again. Desperate to know what new clues and information both Max and Tyne had, she grabbed her keys and headed straight to Barnaby's. Glad that their favorite booth was free, Pearla slid in and was soon joined by Tyne who set down a tray with three iced teas and a basket of breadsticks.

Minutes later, Max showed up and shimmied into the booth next to Tyne. Pearla got straight to business, asking her, "What the heck did Pete Worley want?"

Max shared what she'd found out. "He tried to nail me down regarding Char's interest in the property." She tapped her fingers on the table. "Here's what's interesting. He said they were finalizing the deal in the next few days, so if my friend is indeed interested, she should have her agent get in touch immediately with an offer. I said it wouldn't be possible, that I'd spoken with Char and she simply wasn't comfortable completing a transaction that substantial while out of the country, let alone having not even seen the property in person. Then I asked him why there was such a rush to get the deal done, like, didn't they want to entertain all possible offers?"

"Ooh, how'd he react?" Pearla wanted to know.

"He basically said it was none of my business. It was a family matter that needed to be resolved as quickly as possible."

"Sounds like he needs the money," Pearla said.

"Exactly what I thought, but I was hoping to get more information. I asked him what he thought about all the trespassing that goes on there, and the illegal activity."

"Good one," Pearla agreed, admiring Max for her quick thinking.

"He didn't take the bait. He just said he'll be glad when it's sold and no longer his problem. Then I said, 'Wait, just one more question. Would your father be okay with the land being developed as residential housing?' That's when he lost his patience and ended the conversation, but not before saying it's not zoned for residential."

"Bummer," Pearla said. "What about Janice? Did the wine work its magic?"

Tyne laughed at that, adding, "Janice does like to talk."

Max responded, "Long story short, Janice did not admit Beth wrote the SMPOV. In fact, she vehemently denied it. Do I believe her? No, but I doubt we'll ever get the full truth. Janice also absolutely believes Annie Worley is alive and is purposely avoiding her family. So, nothing super enlightening."

"Ugh, that's so frustrating that Janice won't admit Beth wrote it. Anything else?" Pearla asked.

"One more thing," Max said. "According to Janice, Seth may have been the one who set fire to the clubhouse years ago, but there's no proof of it."

"Your turn, Tyne. What did our friend Colby have to say?" Both women looked at him expectantly.

Tyne explained he'd used flattery and a feigned interest in the sport of paintballing to encourage Colby to talk.

"Colby said there's a whole underground network of sorts, and the players wear full gear including face coverings so no one knows who's who. And when I showed him the photo you took in Jack's room, he said it was an expensive rifle."

"An actual rifle, or a paintball one?" Max asked.

"He thinks it's for paintballing, but it's been modified. Apparently, you can add attachments to make them more powerful. I thought that was interesting. Could someone have used a modified paintball rifle to shoot, say, a golf ball?" Tyne sat back and looked from one to the other.

"Tyne, I think you're on to something. The problem is, it feels like everyone in town is a paintballer and they're all so secretive about it." Max sighed. "In the end, we may just end up watching the property get sold to the highest bidder. Then we'll have to hope that large-scale development isn't allowed."

"Don't give up so easily, Max. Remember, there are tons of restrictions on how that land can be used. That's probably why the Worleys are having trouble unloading it," Tyne said.

"Wait, didn't you say you spoke with the middle Worley brother?" Pearla asked. Tyne nodded.

"Yes, Evan Worley. He was always the most mellow of the bunch from what I remember. He stopped in for a beer just as I opened today. I started reminiscing about my teen years exploring and camping out on the property. We laughed a bit, and then I brought up Annie, saying I heard she was coming back to town. I wanted to gauge his reaction."

Pearla's eyes widened. "Nice move, Tyne. How did Evan react?"

"Neutral. Evan admitted Annie contacted them, but he said she has no plans to return. I asked him if she cared about the sale and he said she doesn't. But the scuttlebutt at the bar last night was that Annie is against the sale and doesn't want the land developed at all." Tyne turned to Pearla, grinning. "What are you laughing at, Pearla?"

Pearla stifled another chuckle. "Sorry, Tyne, I had trouble focusing after hearing you use the term scuttlebutt." Max laughed too and Tyne joined in. When they caught their breath, they sat quietly for a moment, before Max spoke up.

"Tyne, if Annie were to show up, would you recognize her?"

"I'd be able to recognize her, sure. She can't have changed that much."

"Do you think she could be dangerous?"

"Not the Annie I knew."

"Okay, my turn," Pearla said. "I overheard Briggs and Fields talking about teaming up and low-balling the Worleys to buy the property."

"So it's just money-grubbing rich men, wanting to take advantage of another opportunity to get even richer." Max sighed, resting her head in her hands.

"It might be just that, but I think there's something we're missing." Pearla mused, even though she couldn't see a clear connection to the deaths of the other two men. "Hmm," Tyne responded. "I wonder if Briggs and Fields planned this all along ... or if they're simply seizing an opportunity. Could they have staged that conversation to make it look as if they just teamed up?"

"Now that you mention it, it's possible." Pearla remembered how loudly and smugly the men had spoken, almost as if they wanted her to overhear them.

"We should move them up on the suspect list," Max said.

"Yes, we will." Pearla agreed. "And we don't have to sit passively and watch the land get sold. There are efforts we can make." Max smiled and sat up straight.

"We can team up and get the townspeople involved. I bet they'd be willing to protest a housing development. If the investors know the people won't go down without a fight, they might back out and leave, saying it's too much trouble."

Tyne nodded and added, "And that opens the door for the Conservancy to step in and purchase the land if the brothers insist on selling. It's what's best for the town."

Pearla felt her anxiety lessen. She was simply incapable of remaining passive and appreciated having a plan and some next steps in place.

"Well, if that's it for now, I should get back to work," Tyne said. Max slid out of the booth, so he could leave.

"Thanks for your help, Tyne. We appreciate it," Max opened her purse and pulled a twenty from her wallet to pay for the teas and breadsticks.

"Put your money away. This was a meeting of the minds. The snacks are on the house."

Both women thanked him and left through the back door to the parking lot.

"Oh, Max. I forgot to tell you we have a new guest coming tomorrow. It was an odd interaction."

"How so?"

Pearla filled her in. Max's take was that the lady was probably a bit eccentric, nothing more.

Chapter 21

Thursday
Sheriff Silva

Thank goodness for Janice and her well-intentioned nosiness, conveniently right next door. Rene Silva had some specific questions and hoped he could count on Janice as his reliable source for answers. There wasn't exactly an open investigation as he'd inferred to Maxine. There was nothing to investigate. The golf ball accident was just that. He could see no plausible way to identify who had shot the golf ball and whether it had been on purpose. Everyone he'd questioned had denied being on the property. This town's residents protected their own. No one was talking.

He'd even questioned Colby and had gotten exactly

nowhere. What he had found out from his own research was that Seth Worley played golf for his college team and that Evan and Pete had served as Marines, both having dropped out of college, and were excellent marksmen. Interesting, but ultimately circumstantial at best.

It was the same story with the death of Jason Martinez. Tragic. Had a driver deliberately run him off the road? Sure looked that way, but without a witness or cameras, the only facts were that a man was riding his bike on the highway, went over the side of a substantial ditch, and succumbed to fatal injuries. People on the neighborhood app had plenty of remarks about the bike accident, but nothing useful, all condolences and some blaming the fact there was a deep ditch there.

He'd questioned the three Worley brothers together and separately before they lost their patience with him.

"Look, we're only trying to sell our family's land, which we have every right to do. Any accidents are strictly coincidental and not our concern. If there isn't anything else and you have nothing to charge us with, please leave us alone and find a more productive way to spend your time." Pete Junior was the self-appointed spokesman for the brothers.

Only a small-town cop would be expected to take this kind of abuse from the very people he was charged with protecting.

Rene pulled out his notes from the interviews of the Worley brothers and went through them. Seth Worley was a talker. Before Rene had asked any direct questions, Seth had made a show of sympathy for both of the dead men, and had mentioned that the land always made him uncomfortable. *What was it he'd said?* Rene had written "cursed" in his notes, and that jogged his memory. Seth had said there were rumors of the land being cursed. He didn't believe it himself, but was glad to be getting rid of it.

Rene wasn't interested in fairy tales, so he steered the conversation to what mattered, asking Seth directly, "Where were you when Bruce Taylor was killed?" Rene watched Seth's expression change, noticing he clenched his jaw before answering.

"I was held up. I was at the house."

"Held up in what way? And can anyone corroborate that?"

"My brothers can."

"Your brothers weren't with you. They were at the property."

"They knew I was here. I forgot the time. I got distracted."

"Distracted? Wasn't this appointment important enough to remember?" Rene had pressed.

"Look, I have attention deficit disorder. It's always been a real problem for me. I forget things all the time."

Rene had let it go at that point, noting Seth didn't have a solid alibi for the time in question. Seth went on to explain that he hoped to sell the land to the conservancy so it could remain wild. Why keep paying taxes on a huge property no one in the family was interested in? Seth expressed this was the simplest solution and the only one that Annie, his estranged sister, would approve of. Rene pondered the conversation. It made a lot of sense. The youngest brother was motivated to unload the property. And to leave it as-is.

Next, Rene had questioned Evan. The middle brother was the most non-committal of the three. He didn't seem to have any opinion on whom to sell to and would be glad to get his cut and walk away. He didn't know why Seth had missed the meeting, only that he hadn't shown up. Rene had sensed there was no love lost there. Evan had not mentioned Annie at all.

Pete Junior was the last brother Rene had interviewed. Rene had asked him where Seth was at the time of Bruce Taylor's death, and he'd responded, "Didn't he tell you he was at the house?" Rene had said yes. Then he asked Pete his thoughts on selling to the conservancy.

"Seth is harping on that because he doesn't want the land disturbed," Pete said.

"Do you think he's trying to do what your sister wants?" Rene had asked.

"My sister? You mean Annie?" Pete had laughed scornfully at this. "Sheriff, I believe my sister is dead. No one has heard from her for over seven years."

"What about the message she sent?"

"I don't think she sent it."

"Who do you think did?"

"No idea. Maybe someone's idea of a cruel joke. Look, I care about my brothers, and I want to do what's best. We need to get this property sold and walk away. I'm fine unloading it to whoever gives us a fair price, including the conservancy. I'm sorry that man died, but it has nothing at all to do with me or my brothers. Period. And I think you know that, Sheriff."

Max and Pearla made it clear they thought the deaths were somehow planned and related, and they'd found out through the grapevine that Annie Worley had contacted her brothers. Janice confirmed Annie has a post box, and she believes wholeheartedly Annie isn't dead. The entire population of Silvermist is willing to accept at face value that Annie disappeared seven years ago, right before her father's death and has not been seen or heard from since, until this out-of-the-blue text exchange with her brothers.

Janice suggested he take it easy when he brought up the possibility that Annie was no longer alive, calling it hogwash.

"Where does Annie fit into her brothers' selling of the land? Wouldn't she care about getting her slice of the pie?" he'd asked Janice.

She'd fixed him with a look. "How many ways can I tell you? Annie left town on purpose and renounced her place in the family. She was never interested in the money."

"I don't buy it." Rene couldn't get his head around someone refusing their part of an inheritance. He never would.

"Just to be clear, Annie left before her father died?"

"Yes, I told you that already."

"And she did not attend the funeral?"

"No, she did not. Why are we going over this again, Sheriff?"

"Pete Senior's body was found quite some time after he died, though. Didn't a neighbor find him?"

"Yes."

Apparently, I will need to spell this out.

"Janice, is it not suspicious that Annie left town? And that Pete Senior was found at the bottom of the stairs in his home a week or more after his actual death?" He paused, hoping to let her ponder the question, before adding, "Maybe she killed him."

Janice had the nerve to laugh. "You've never seen Annie, or met her. She did not push her father down the stairs. She's a frail little thing. And she sent a beautiful wreath to the funeral."

"So you've said. Well, thanks for your help, Janice."

When she left the office, he closed the door. Rene had pulled the autopsy report for Pete Worley Sr. which listed the cause of death as injuries sustained from a fall. *Did he fall, or could he have been pushed?*

The older man had succumbed to injuries, with no one near to help him. What a terrible way to die.

Chapter 22

Max

What time do you think Hannah Smith will arrive?"
Max asked Pearla, as they walked the grounds of the
inn with Larry Trawl. One of the guests had mentioned the
pool filter was making a strange noise and Larry wanted to
examine it. On the opposite side of the pool, Nolan Briggs
waved from a sun lounger, then slowly removed his shirt,
pulling it over his head.

"Yuck," Pearla said under her breath. There were
several dark bruised marks on his pale white skin.

"Sorry, but look again," Max whispered. "Aren't those
bruises?" Pearla's eyes went wide.

"Like the kind of bruises one would get from getting
shot with paintballs?"

"They certainly could be."

Larry was distracted, examining the pool filter while Max and Pearla stood by. "I think a little adjustment is all it needs," he said confidently. "You don't need a replacement yet. I'll keep an eye on it, though. And I'll have Colby get a price on a new one."

"Thanks, Larry. We appreciate your expertise. We couldn't get along without you."

Larry smiled his approval, and Max asked, "Larry, you remember the Worley family. Do you think you would recognize Annie Worley if you saw her in person? I know it's been a while since she left Silvermist."

Larry nodded. "I believe I'd recognize her, yes. She can't have changed too much. Do you think she'll come back?"

"Honestly, Larry, I don't know what to think."

* * *

Max sat at the office computer and searched 'Morehouse Developments'. The results showed large-scale projects including entire neighborhoods. Further digging revealed lawsuits they'd been involved in. In one instance, the company had built on previously protected wetlands. Max sighed deeply. They had gotten away with it several times— purchased land with limited development potential, such as land deemed agricultural or environmentally sensitive, and had developed it anyway.

She whispered to Butters, who was curled up in one of his many plush donut beds, "So they're buying up land for pennies on the dollar because it's not zoned for development. Then they get it rezoned afterwards, or they simply pay the penalties. And profit big time." Butters gave her a wide stare and let out a small meow. *I think I'm onto something.*

Max was loath to think Misty knew about Jack's plans and had lied to her. Misty had gone to the property meeting pretending she might be interested, to help Max. The last they'd spoken was the day of Jason Martinez's death. *Could I have misread her?* Max had to find the truth. She needed to ask Misty if she was involved with Jack romantically, while not admitting to snooping in Jack's room. Redness crept up her neck to her cheeks. She was not proud of the snooping. She picked up her phone and sent Misty a text before she could change her mind.

Up for a bike ride?

Sure, when?

How's 4?

Perfect

Max closed the screen on her phone and shut down her computer. She was fidgety and needed to move her body. She considered a walk to the shoreline, but with Pearla making a run into Brookhaven, she wanted to stick close by. Someone needed to be present to check in Hannah Smith.

As she stood up and stretched, her eyes caught the belongings of the two deceased men, which were still stacked in the corner. Sheriff Silva had not asked about the men's personal effects, and she made a mental note to call him later to deal with it.

Had the men been alive, both of their reservations would end as of Saturday, with new guests checking in to the rooms. The concern about messing with the belongings was evidently unfounded. The rooms had already been cleaned and had sat vacant since the incidents. She shooed

Butters out and closed the office door, checking the handle to confirm it was securely locked.

A stroll through the grounds had Max feeling calmer and reminded her of how blessed she was to call this place home. It truly was a dream realized. She noticed Nolan Briggs was still sitting in the shade by the pool. Thankfully, he'd put his shirt back on. J.T. Fields had pulled another sun lounger over and was next to him. Without thinking, Max approached the two men.

"Hello. Are you both enjoying your stay?" They nodded and thanked her. Max grabbed a single chair near them and carried it over while asking, "Mind if I join you?"

There was no opportunity for the men to object without looking like jerks. Nolan Briggs, ever the gentleman and hardly containing his annoyance, said, "We were having an important meeting, but sure."

Max cut straight to the matter. No need to worry about them making a return visit to the inn if she offended them. "Are either of you planning to develop the Worley property if you purchase it?"

Nolan Briggs cocked his head and smirked, while J.T. Fields cleared his throat before responding, "That's presumptuous. Why are you asking us this?"

Max had not prepared what to say. She hadn't known she was even going to speak to them, but seeing them looking so smug annoyed her and she wondered which would be the best angle, the innocent and curious ask, or the more forceful, I'm onto you, approach. In an instant, she chose the latter.

"Look, gentleman. As a community member of Silvermist Point, I'm concerned about what will become of the property once it changes hands. Mind you, I'm not only speaking for myself. Our community is strong here, and we will not allow extensive development without a major fight." Max was proud of her quick improvisation.

"Whoa, hold up. First, it is none of your business what happens to land in the hands of a private owner. You and your neighbors don't get to decide," Briggs responded with barely controlled anger, betrayed by his scarlet face.

"And second," Fields piped up, "you have a lot of nerve inserting yourself into our private conversation."

"Oh, your conversation?" Max asked. "It's interesting that you two are having such an intimate and cozy talk, what with you being in competition and all." She let that sink in, standing up and putting her hands on her hips. *I'm not letting these two men intimidate me on my own grounds.*

"And third," Briggs sputtered, "I don't know where you get your information, but no one said anything about extensive development."

"I know that's what you want people to believe, and I'm here to tell you, I hope it's true. Or there will be major pushback. Trust me."

Neither man spoke for a beat; they stared at her. Uncomfortable, and wanting to dial back the tension, Max added, "This place is special. We want to keep it that way. Sorry for getting so worked up, but I care deeply about what happens here. I can only hope whoever buys the land will too." Max watched their stern faces relax to neutral.

"Sure, okay. My wife gets fired up about things too. Things over which she has no control. I understand," Briggs said.

What a gem!

Max could only nod, though she had many retorts threatening to spew forth. She had let her emotions take over, but how could she not? The thought of some careless, money-hungry developer thoughtlessly changing the landscape of her beloved home got her fired up. She walked back to her cottage, unsure if she'd accomplished anything by that interaction and wishing she'd kept her mouth shut.

Butters crept out from under one of the bushes lining the walkway. His silky fur was covered in small bits of leaves and twigs. He flipped onto his back and lolled on the walkway in front of her, blocking her path. Max picked him up and hugged him to her chest. He was warm and cuddly and in need of a good brushing.

Her phone vibrated in her pocket. She checked it, an alert from the front desk. Setting Butters down gently, she turned and walked back toward the inn. As she rounded the front of the building, Larry called to her. She looked at him as he held a double thumbs-up, then cocked his head toward the front entrance.

"We can chat in a few minutes, Larry. I need to check in our guest first." Max hurried into the reception area.

Her first view of their new guest was from the back. She was petite, barely five feet tall, and she had on a long coat—beige and of light material, but still too heavy for the warm afternoon. Her hair, light brown, peeked out from under a round felt hat. It was trimmed in a precise straight line and fell to her mid-shoulders. When she turned around, Max saw tinted glasses that were far too large for her face. Her expression was tense, her lips closed tightly.

Max smiled warmly. "Welcome to the inn. You must be Hannah Smith, is that correct?"

"Yes," the woman replied, then appeared to be waiting, so Max spoke up again, hoping to put her at ease.

"My name's Maxine Egan, but everyone calls me Max. I bought the inn from the Evanses. Pearla, whom you spoke with on the phone, tells me you knew the Evanses. Did you grow up in Silvermist Point?"

Hannah's eyes darted around nervously, and she pushed her too-large glasses up on her nose. "No. I, um, stayed here once. That's how I knew Mable Evans. I must have given your receptionist the wrong impression."

"I understand, and I didn't mean to pry. I can show you to your room; I have you booked in the suite. I'll just need a credit card for incidentals. Nothing will be charged until you check out."

"No. I was told that wouldn't be necessary. I said I'd pay in cash and I can pay up front if you need."

What a nervous bird.

"Alright then, we can do that. Why don't you pay for the first night, and we can square up for the remainder when you check out?"

Relief washed over Hannah's face. She opened her purse and rummaged through it, pulling out a thick roll of bills held together with a rubber band.

"We normally ask to run a copy of your driver's license for our file. Would you mind?" Max knew she would mind. The scared rabbit look came out, and the woman's eyes filled, as if she might burst into tears. Max almost felt sorry for her, but waited patiently for the woman's response. She wouldn't let her off the hook so easily.

"I don't have a valid ID; I lost it. And I'm waiting for a new one to be mailed. I'm sure you understand; Mable would have."

Max turned and grabbed the brass key to the room and the electronic key card for the common areas before responding. "No worries, Ms. Smith. I'll show you to your room. It's just upstairs."

The woman let out a breath in a sigh and thanked Max for her understanding.

"I'm sure the room will be fine. I'll get my luggage from my rental car, and you can point me in the right direction." Max longed to ask how it was possible to rent a car with no ID or credit card, but held her tongue.

"Let me get our maintenance man to help you," she said as she followed her out the front door and down the steps.

"Ms. Smith, this is Mr. Trawl. He will assist you with your belongings."

"Okay, well thank you," she said and took a step back. Larry removed his gloves and hefted the suitcase from the trunk. For an old man, his strength was impressive.

"Just follow me, Miss. Your room is upstairs."

"There's a phone in your room. You can use it to call if there's anything you need. Also, there's a reception from four-thirty to six right here in the living room. I hope you'll enjoy your stay with us." Max turned to leave.

"Thank you, I may just rest a while."

Minutes later, Larry was back downstairs and Max immediately noticed his expression.

"What was it you wanted to tell me, Larry?"

"I wanted to tell you, our guest is Annie Worley." Max gasped. She had sensed something was off with Hannah, but this was unexpected.

"Are you certain?"

"I am. She's wearing a disguise, but I can tell it's her. Beth used to wear disguises from time to time. I'd see her around town and she thought I couldn't recognize her, but I always could." Max recalled the box of wigs she and Pearla had found in Beth's closet.

"Colby knows she's Annie too. He recognized her right when she got out of her rental car. I told him to keep his trap shut."

"Thank you, Larry. You're incredibly helpful."

"No problem." Larry nodded solemnly before walking away.

Chapter 23

Pearla

Stress and excitement surged through Pearla until it felt like all her nerve endings were exposed. The drive back to the inn felt longer than usual as thoughts circulated through her mind. Max had called to tell her that not only was Annie Worley not dead, she was a guest at the Snowy Plover Inn. Pearla hadn't ever believed Annie was dead, even though she struggled to grasp why anyone would abandon their family and not attend their father's funeral. Now she needed to work out exactly why Annie was there. What part did Annie play in this unfolding drama? Why return after ghosting everyone in town for seven years?

Max had explained that Annie was clearly attempting to be in disguise, but that Larry was certain it was her, and he would know. Pearla tried to picture Annie, but could manage to conjure only a vague image. Finally, she pulled into the circular driveway and saw Larry and Colby still working at the front of the property. She rolled down her window and called them over.

"Larry, thank you for your help. Max told me you recognized Annie even with her disguise."

"Well, yes. That was no problem. It's definitely her."

"I saw her too," Colby piped up.

"Well, thank you as well." Pearla smiled. "Hey, would you mind unloading the car for me as soon as I park? I have some supplies in the trunk. Most go in the kitchen pantry, and the rest in the basement."

"Of course. I'll get right on that," Colby said, without any hint of his usual bravado or sarcasm, and it occurred to Pearla that both men enjoyed being needed.

Annie was so close. Now if only she could figure out how to speak with her without being obvious. She thought about simply knocking on her door. Would Annie open it? If she did, how should Pearla kick off the conversation? Pearla let her mind play out scenarios as she made her way to her apartment. Her intention was to immediately add an index card for Annie Worley and work her into the suspect list, though Annie's direct involvement was unlikely if she had just arrived in town.

Pearla took the outside spiral staircase, which led to her apartment's back door and up to the tower. As she looked up, she saw a petite woman in the circular glass room, sitting on the window bench. It had to be Annie. Without pausing to plan, she continued up the stairs and joined the woman in the room. The slight woman visibly startled when Pearla entered, and she snatched up a pair of large tinted glasses from the seat next to her, shoving them on her face. Pearla had caught her off guard.

Stepping closer, Pearla asked her, "Please tell me why you're in disguise. I know who you are, and I don't want any trouble at the inn; there's already been enough. I'm sure you understand."

The expression on Annie's face below the tinted glasses was one of surprise mixed with confusion. She held her hands out in front of her, palms up, as if in surrender. "I have no intention of causing you trouble. Look, you probably don't know much about my family."

"I know you left Silvermist Point years ago," Pearla interrupted without meaning to. "The whole town talks about it."

"Oh, well, Silvermist has always been a difficult place to keep secrets," Annie said cryptically, and she removed the glasses.

"So why the secrecy? I don't get it. And why come back now?" Pearla craved answers.

Annie sighed deeply. "I don't feel safe around my brothers. I won't go into why."

When she heard that admission, Pearla felt anger rising in her chest and she balled her fists. *If those brothers abused her…*

Annie took one look at Pearla's expression and read it correctly. "No, no. It's not what you think. No one ever physically abused me. Nothing like that. More like veiled threats and relentless, mean teasing. I don't trust them, that's all."

Pearla waited expectantly, hoping Annie would keep talking. She did.

"Our family dynamic was toxic. I had to leave. All three

of my brothers were so interested in my parents' estate and what they would inherit. It sickened me. So, I left."

"Is that all?" Pearla couldn't reconcile disappearing for years over a difference of opinion. Lots of people had annoying, selfish siblings; it didn't mean you took off permanently with no forwarding address.

"The one thing my father asked of us after my mother's passing was that we never sell the land on the bluff. His dream was for us, his four children, to build homes there and settle with our families. Silvermist Point was the place we vacationed as kids. We never lived here full time, but it was always my father's dream to settle here permanently. He felt it was magical, he said so all the time."

"I certainly get that." Pearla smiled.

"After Mom passed away, Dad moved here permanently. He said he felt closest to her here." Annie's eyes were watery. Either she was a very skilled actor, or she was sincere.

"What about the golf course?" Pearla asked.

Annie nodded thoughtfully. "The golf course was a pet project of Dad's. He always hoped one of his boys would rebuild it after the clubhouse burned, but no one showed any interest. I'm sorry, I'm rambling." Annie paused again, which gave Pearla a minute to collect her thoughts. She was learning a lot and didn't want to discourage Annie from talking more about her family, specifically her brothers.

"You're not rambling at all. I'm happy to be a sounding board. And just so you know, most of us who live here full time are against the development of the property, other than for a small golf course as it was before. Absolutely no one wants big development." Pearla watched the tension ease from Annie's shoulders. She had said the right thing, and it was the honest truth.

"Thank you, I appreciate that." Annie stood up to stretch and gaze out the tower window toward the shore.

"Before I left for good, Dad had gathered us all here in Silvermist. We were at our family vacation home. It's not far from here. Dad was living there, like I said. That was the last time I saw him or my brothers. It's been more than seven years now. Dad was acting very sentimental, almost as if he believed it was his time to die soon." Annie gazed out toward the ocean.

They mustn't have known he had cancer.

"It was strange and uncomfortable, to be honest. Dad wanted to tell us about his will, and how he was going to change it. He made it very clear he planned to specify that the property on the bluff was never to be sold. We could live there or donate it or create a park space in the family name. I was fine with that and said so, but my brothers weren't. They didn't want my dad to put it in the will. They said they'd honor it, but he didn't need to include it."

"Hmm, that's interesting," Pearla acknowledged.

"All of us would get a substantial inheritance regardless. I didn't get why it mattered."

That explains the rush to sell. But how are they able to sell if it's forbidden in the will? Pearla did not want to stop the flow of the story or the gold mine of information she was learning from Annie. She continued to take mental notes while planning to write down the information later and process it. She regretted not having her phone to record the conversation.

"I'd finally moved away and was doing my own thing and I didn't want the money, nor did I want to think about losing my dad. I was still grieving the loss of my mom and being there with my brothers was uncomfortable and unpleasant. I was sick of my role in the family as the only sister. My entire life, I felt I had something to prove, and I had made some admittedly stupid choices, but finally I was living for myself. So, after a ridiculous fight with my brothers, I announced I was leaving, and I didn't care about Dad's money at all. They could have it."

Annie let out a sarcastic laugh. "I was quite dramatic. I'm embarrassed when I recall it. I think my brothers all left soon after me. They were probably glad to know they could have my share of the family money."

"I bet they were." Pearla could barely keep the sarcasm from her voice.

"Exactly. They cared more about money than anything. Then, a few weeks later, Seth texts me that Dad passed away. I was in Switzerland. It was a shock. He texted me only two days before the funeral. There was no chance I could make it on time. I sent a wreath and went to church. I had my own private funeral and grieved in my own way. The longer I was away, the better I felt about myself and the less I felt the need to ever return or contact my brothers. I could reinvent myself and that is what I did."

"So why now? I don't mean to pry. But why are you back?"

"I learned what was happening from Seth. I think he had a pang of guilt, but he's also afraid Pete and Evan are going to somehow double-cross him on the deal and not honor Dad's wishes. Seth's always had a chip on his shoulder, a major inferiority complex because he's the youngest. He asked me to intervene, so I sent a group text."

"But isn't Seth going against your dad too? I thought the will stipulated you can't sell."

"The will was never changed, apparently. Everyone was

fine with honoring my father's wishes until they needed the money. I figure Seth is trying to ease his own conscience, by at least trying to sell to someone who would only build a golf course or to a preservation society."

"We keep hearing it's only zoned for that."

"Supposedly, but maybe it can be changed. Like I said, I don't trust them."

"I don't blame you."

Then Annie surprised her by asking, "You said you didn't want any more trouble at the inn. What did you mean by that?" Pearla wasn't sure how much detail to give, but her gut told her to trust Annie.

"Annie, two of the four potential investors have died somewhat suspiciously. Both were staying at the inn."

Annie gasped, and put her hand to her heart. "I can't imagine my brothers would be connected to anyone dying," she said.

Unless she was faking it, this seemed to be a surprise to Annie. "I'm not implying they are."

"But I also wouldn't have believed they'd betray my father, so…" Annie's shoulders slumped and Pearla saw desperation in her eyes.

Pearla had a wild idea and blurted it out before considering the possibilities. "Have you thought about talking to your brothers directly? I can go with you so you're not alone. It couldn't hurt to talk. They must need your approval to sell, once they know you're back in town, so they're going to want to convince you."

Annie's eyes lit up. "You would do that? You hardly know me."

"I want to help you."

"Thank you. I should probably consult with a lawyer

before I approach my brothers. I can have the lawyer contact them and make it clear that no sale can go through without my approval. That should stall them."

"Good," Pearla felt relieved that the sale would be suspended at least temporarily.

"I still have my key to the house. This might sound strange, but I'd like to go in when no one's there and snoop around before I talk to any of them, before they know I'm here." Annie looked sheepishly at Pearla.

"Wise idea, and I'm happy to come along. We can stake out the house tomorrow morning to make sure they all leave. Then we'll go in."

"Your confidence is putting me at ease, Pearla."

"I do like a good challenge."

Chapter 24

Max

Max eased one of the beach cruisers out of the bicycle parking rack. She checked her watch. Max had seen Misty arrive at the inn earlier, but Misty had gone straight to her room and hadn't texted her yet. She didn't want the interaction to feel awkward, but finding Misty's scarf in Jack's room had made her feel all kinds of awkward.

Did Misty know about Jack's plans to buy the property out from under the other investors? Did she know what Jack and his uncle's development company were planning to do with the property?

"Be right there," Misty called out in her usual cheery voice. Max took a deep breath to steady her nerves. This should be interesting. Misty came around the corner, polished as always with not a hair out of place. The light and airy turquoise scarf Max had seen in Jack's room hung loosely around her neck.

"I just love that scarf. It goes so well with your coloring," Max said.

"Oh, this?" Misty waved the end of the light material. "Funny story about this scarf. I left it in Jack's room, and he just returned it to me today." Misty rolled out a beach cruiser and swung her leg over the seat, preparing to ride. Max was shocked. Had Misty just admitted to being in Jack's room? Yuck.

"What were you doing in Jack's room?" Max couldn't help herself.

"We were discussing a problem with the dining room layout at the spa. I swear, I never knew the level of detail it takes for a project this big."

Max was ashamed for thinking Misty and Jack might be having a secret love affair.

"Oh, so there's been a lot of delays? Do you think you'll make the deadline to open in spring?"

Misty rolled her eyes and sighed. "Let's ride for a bit, and I'll tell you all about it. I've had a rough day. If I don't get some exercise, I might explode."

Max wondered what Misty was upset about. It didn't seem like she knew about Jack's plans; at least that was comforting. Max followed behind Misty as she weaved her way through the neighborhood streets, then gradually uphill. It was too tricky to hold a conversation this way, and Max knew she would need to wait a little longer to satisfy her curiosity. But she was not sensing a vibe that Misty was lying to her. If Misty was lying, she was skilled.

After riding through the streets and out to the bluff,

Misty pulled over. She jumped off her bike and took a sip from her water bottle. Max did the same. They were at one of the public areas where you could walk up to the edge of the bluff and admire the endless view of the Pacific.

"I needed this." Misty took in deep breaths of the cool, salty air.

"Anything you want to talk about?" Max prompted.

"I'm calming down, but I am still livid. You will not believe what Jack did."

"Jack? What did he do?" Max asked casually, not wanting to reveal her current feelings of animosity toward Jack.

"He said he might need to quit the project, that's what." Misty's eyes were filled with anxiety and Max felt instant sympathy, relieved to learn Misty had no part in Jack's duplicity.

"I'm so sorry, Misty. When did he tell you? Did he explain why?"

"Just today. He was frustratingly vague. So now I fear I can't trust him. He claims an opportunity he can't refuse came up, and if it works out, he's going to take it. Can you believe it? The man has no integrity. I'm so angry. The job isn't done, and I don't know how I could replace him this far into the project. The worst part is he wasn't even remorseful. I'm ashamed to say I wanted to slap him, slap the arrogant expression off his face. I swear, Max, you think you know someone. What am I going to do?"

"I should have told you sooner," Max blurted.

"Told me what?"

"Pearla and I saw Jack at the Worley property. We weren't supposed to be there, but we snuck in. It's easy to get in; everyone does it."

"Oh."

Max was unable to tell by her expression if she was upset with her for not telling her sooner. "Yes, well, we saw Jack with a couple of other men. They were taking measurements and walking around. We didn't get close enough to hear exactly what they were talking about."

"Well, what does this have to do with him quitting?"

"I'm not sure. It just looked super suspicious. My friend, Char, knows how to dig stuff up online, so I had her do a search on him. Turns out Jack's uncle has an investment company that's known for some very lucrative, but very shady business deals. We thought Jack might try to strike a deal to buy the Worley property."

"Ah, and now that he told me about this 'opportunity', it looks like you're right," Misty said.

Max had purposely omitted the details of her and Pearla sneaking into Jack's room and finding the development plans and Misty's scarf.

"Max, do you think Jack might have something to do with those other potential investors dying?"

"I don't know, do you? You know him better."

"I thought I knew him, but now I have my doubts. What should we do? Should we tell Sheriff Silva?"

"Let's ride over to the village and check if he's in his office. If he's there, we'll talk to him."

"Sounds like a plan."

Within ten minutes, they were back in the village. They wheeled the bikes into the Mail Stop and put the kickstands down. Janice was behind the counter and scowled her disapproval at the bikes.

"Hi Janice, I didn't bring locks, and I don't want to leave the bikes out front on the sidewalk. Can we park them here just for a few minutes?"

"That will be fine for a few minutes."

"Is the sheriff in?" Misty asked with sweetness and light. "I had a concern."

Janice's face lit up at that. "Yes, he's in his office."

"Great, we'll only be a few minutes, I promise."

Janice nodded. Max could feel Janice's eyes on her back as she walked across the small shop and tapped on the slightly ajar door.

"Sheriff Silva?" she called.

"Come on in." Rene looked up from his computer and shoved a stack of papers aside, then stood, smiling. "Hello, Max, we meet again."

Max stepped inside, followed by Misty, who did not fully shut the door. "Yes, and I've brought Misty Caldwell. She's the owner of the Getaway Ranch. Have you two met?"

"I think so, yes," Misty said. "But you might not remember me."

"Yes, I do." Rene held out his hand and Misty shook it.

No man was likely not to remember meeting Misty Caldwell.

"Have a seat. How can I help you?"

Max took a breath and proceeded to relay what they had learned about Jack. All the while, Rene jotted down notes on his pad. When she paused, he looked up, seeming to wait for her to speak more. When she didn't, he asked, "What do you think I should do with this information, Max?"

"I think you should consider that Jack has no alibi for the times of the two suspicious deaths. It's worth following up."

"How do you know he has no alibi?" Rene asked, clearly intrigued, but trying not to show it.

"I don't know where he was exactly, but I do know he was not on the job site during those times," Misty said. "And what if he's involved with the deaths of those two men? I think it's worth exploring."

Max was trying to read Rene's expression as Misty spoke. "On another subject, is there anything we can do as citizens to stop the sale of the Worley property?"

Rene stopped writing notes. He placed his elbows on the edge of his desk and steepled his fingers. After a brief pause, he responded. "Ok, Ms. Caldwell, it seems you have two different concerns. Here's what I can do. I will question Jack to see if he has an alibi for those times. As far as the sale, there's nothing I can personally do, but there's power in numbers. If word were to get out that the property might get developed more than originally intended or legally allowed, people would have something to say about it."

Max heard Janice cough loudly right outside the door.

"Thank you, Sheriff, I appreciate your help. I'm glad Max encouraged me to speak with you," Misty said as she stood.

"And thanks for your thoughtful advice," Max added. "I think spreading the word might be the answer to stopping any chance of big development, before it even becomes a consideration." In her mind, she pictured the rows and rows of homes on the bluff and tried not to shudder at the mental image.

When they stepped out of the office, Janice was busily straightening items behind the counter. Max thought about asking her for help with getting the word out about the property development, but figured it would be more effective to let Janice run with it on her own, as if it was her idea in the first place.

"Thanks for letting us park the bikes here," Misty called out, while rolling hers out the door.

"Yes, thanks, Janice. I'm looking forward to having lunch again soon," Max said and watched a grin spread across Janice's face.

"I'd be delighted. Just say when."

Chapter 25

Friday
Pearla

Pearla and Annie sat in Annie's rental car just down the hill from the Worley family home.

"I never knew a stakeout could be this delicious," Annie joked, as she took a bite of a warm chocolate croissant from Front Porch Bakery.

Both ladies were in disguise. Annie with her wig and tinted oversized glasses and Pearla in a black hoodie and dark glasses. The car was parked on the right side of the road, providing them a clear view of who drove down the hill.

Pearla sipped her coffee. "The Front Porch Bakery never disappoints," she said. "Look, here comes an SUV."

They watched it pass. There were two men in the front seat. Pearla recognized Pete and Evan Worley, but the rear windows were tinted making it impossible to tell if anyone else was seated in the backseat.

"They're probably all together, grabbing breakfast. None of them like to cook," Annie reasoned. "Let's go for it."

Pearla had her doubts, but nodded okay. "We should move the car closer, but not park in the driveway. Too obvious if they come back. Also, we should make sure no one's home before we go in."

"Good idea," Annie agreed. She parked closer. They walked around and approached the house from the back. None of the lights were on, and it certainly appeared empty. Annie took her key from her pocket and tried it in the back door. After wiggling it, the lock clicked.

"Still works," she said and pushed open the door. They stepped in and closed it. Annie flicked on the lights and they looked around. They were in the kitchen. It was still as messy, if not more so than it had been the other day when Pearla peeked in the front window.

"I'm going to check out my old room," Annie said. "But you can see if there's anything interesting in here."

Pearla felt like Annie had read her mind. She was confident she could uncover something incriminating here. The question was what? She scanned the room. What a cool vacation home. She pictured happy Worley family gatherings.

There were papers on the coffee table in the great room and Pearla rifled through them, not knowing what she might uncover. One stapled stack had information on the zoning of the property along with an aerial map similar to the one she'd seen in Jason Martinez's room. Nothing else stood out, and Pearla continued her exploration.

The first door she tried led to what she guessed was the master suite, a huge bedroom with its own fireplace and sitting area, as well as an attached bathroom. It was obvious from the rumpled bed and clothes thrown on the floor that one of the brothers was using this room. She figured it was Pete, the oldest. A quick examination of the walk-in closet, and she learned no one had ever cleared the home of Pete Senior's belongings in all the years since he passed. There was even a fair amount of Mrs. Worley's clothing in the closet, and Pearla was surprised to feel a wave of sadness. She paused to say a quick prayer for the repose of their souls.

Only half of the bed had been slept in, and Pearla tried the drawer of the nightstand. A Bible, a package of tissues, and a pair of glasses. Then her hand felt something at the back of the drawer — a narrow rectangular box. It held two camouflage golf balls; an empty spot revealed the third ball was missing, and Pearla guessed it was the one she'd fished from Chief's slobbery mouth. If the missing ball had been used to murder Bruce Taylor, did that mean Pete Jr. was connected to the crime?

Pearla located Annie two doors down sitting on her childhood trundle bed. It was a twin frame with a bubblegum pink frilly bedspread and some stuffed animals which had seen better days.

"I found my old journal," Annie announced. "Just where I hid it. I must've been like fourteen." She held up a red Hello Kitty journal. It was similar to the one Pearla had as a young teen. "It's like a time capsule of my youth in here."

Pearla didn't want to spend too much time reminiscing.

They didn't know when Annie's brothers would return.

"Annie, do you think we can find your father's legal documents here, a copy of his will, maybe?"

"We all have copies. We've had them since before he passed. There's nothing in the will that can help us. Remember, my dad never changed it before he died. If my brothers want to force the sale of the property, they can. It's just that they'll have a harder time if I object." The distinct sound of a car engine interrupted their conversation.

"Did you hear that?" Pearla whispered and pointed to the front window. "I think a car just pulled up. Should we hide?" Annie stepped over to the window. "A red Jeep. It's Seth. He's alone. I'm going to tell him I'm here. I think he's safe; we've always been close."

With no time to protest or consider if Annie was making a safe decision, Pearla asked, "What should I do?"

"Follow me." Annie led Pearla to the front room and directed her to a large closet. Pearla could hear the door of the Jeep slamming. In seconds, Seth Worley would be in the house. There simply wasn't time to think of alternatives. Beads of sweat formed on her forehead at the thought of a confrontation. She slipped into the closet, and Annie closed the door.

"Stay here and stay silent. You can listen in and call for help if anything gets weird."

"What are you gonna…" Pearla couldn't finish the thought as the front door opened and Seth Worley entered the house. All she could do was hope Annie was correct in thinking Seth wasn't dangerous and wouldn't harm her.

"Seth," Annie said quietly. Pearla heard him jump and take in a sharp breath.

"Whoa, what the heck? Annie is that you?" He crossed

the room with heavy steps.

"Oh my gosh, it's been forever. What are you wearing? Is that a wig?"

"I didn't want anyone from the village to recognize me." Annie let out a nervous giggle. "Seth, what is going on? You guys know darn well Dad didn't want our family property sold. What are you thinking? Why are you going along with it?"

Pearla could hear every word clearly. She was less than ten feet away, and the closet had louver blinds. She was careful not to move and possibly cast a shadow. Annie might trust her brother, but Pearla did not.

"I don't know what you've been up to all these years, Annie, thanks to the fact that you've made no effort to communicate, but all of us need the money. I'm trying to at least honor Dad's wish by having the new owner restore the nine-hole golf course. I wanted to sell it to a conservancy, but we'd never get the amount a private investor would pay, so Pete won't agree."

"What about Evan?" Annie paused for a second, but not long enough to give Seth the opportunity to respond. "Never mind, Evan always did whatever Pete wanted. I see nothing has changed."

"They're both good guys, Annie. You'll see. It's not fair of you to judge. You can't say you know them after all this time." Pearla heard Annie sigh and through the louvers could see that Seth was in constant motion.

"Did you have a crisis of conscience? Are you regretting you didn't take over the golf course before it burned down so unexpectedly? Is that why you emailed me?" Annie asked.

Is she insinuating he burned it?

"About the clubhouse," Seth started. "No, never mind. And there isn't a crisis. What we are doing is perfectly justified. I'm fully onboard with the sale. We have to do it. I wanted to find you so you could get your share."

"I still don't care about the money, Seth. I care about loyalty to Dad," Annie pleaded.

"You'd understand better if you had kids of your own and knew how expensive they are. Dad cannot expect us to conform to his wishes from the grave. I had no way of getting in touch with you until recently, or I would have. I've missed you, Sis, and I can't believe you're here, and alive." His voice was wrought with emotion.

Is he faking it?

"I made Janice promise not to give out my information, but I guess she made the right decision to give it to you," Annie said, sounding like tears were threatening.

"Believe me, I had to beg her to give it up. You always ignored my texts so I figured you ditched that number. I'm glad you saw the email."

"So, what happens now? Can we convince them to stop the sale?" Pearla heard the pleading in Annie's voice. Seth huffed out a breath. His steps echoed on the wood floor as he paced.

"No, Annie, like I said, the sale is happening. Evan and I met with two investors last night. They've teamed up, and they gave us a number. It's not what we hoped for, but we have no choice at this point. Truth is, we are all in terrible financial shape. Bad investments, Pete's divorce, and Evan's kids are ready for college. It's a mess. We have to sell."

"Well, I object," Annie said. "You can't do it without my approval."

"We can, Annie. And it's all but settled. Evan and I

plan to work out the details together with Pete, and we'll sign later today. Don't worry, we'll honor your share."

"I already said I don't want the money. Hey, why don't you sell the house instead?"

"We had it appraised and it's not enough. You can have it if you want."

Oh, how generous of you.

"Actually, I'd have to clear that with Pete and Evan," Seth backtracked.

"You're letting them push you around, just like you always have. I'm disappointed in you, Seth."

Pearla was quietly absorbing all this in the hideout of the closet. For once, she was glad she had no siblings of her own to quarrel with.

"Nobody is pushing me around, Annie, it's not like that. We're all adults, making a mutual decision. Come here, let's hug this out."

Pearla heard Annie sigh again before walking over to Seth and accepting his hug. Pearla had to force herself not to emit a loud groan. *Why did Annie give in so easily?*

"I'm sorry," Seth said, his voice full of emotion. "I don't want to hurt you. Let's all sit down and work it out like a family should. I'll call Pete and Evan right now. They'll be pleased you're here."

"No, don't. I'm not ready for that," Annie said. "Can you please not let Pete and Evan know I'm in town? I need time to process this."

"Sure. I can respect that," Seth agreed. "I'm going to hit some balls on the property and give it a walk through before it's not ours anymore. I came here to grab my clubs. Hey, do you want to come with me?"

"No, not now," Annie said. "I'll call you later. Maybe

then I'll be ready to face Pete and Evan."

Pearla heard Seth rummage around before leaving and was thankful his golf clubs were not in the closet with her. As soon as she heard his car door slam, Pearla pushed open the closet door and joined Annie on the sofa where she sat, defeated, holding her head in her hands and brushing tears away with her sleeve.

"That was rough," Pearla said. "I know it's not the response you were hoping for."

"I'm sorry, Pearla. I don't agree with what they're doing, but it sure looks like there's no choice but to let it happen. I can't buy them out of the property. I don't have the means. If only my father had the chance to change his will before he died."

"Yes, that's really too bad," Pearla agreed, but she was distracted by another thought.

Annie's father had died after Annie left. Unfortunate, but also convenient. When had her brothers left? Pete Worley Senior's cause of death was recorded as injuries sustained from falling down the stairs, but might he have been pushed? She couldn't very well ask Annie outright, but maybe she should. Before she could talk herself out of it, Pearla walked over to the staircase that led downward.

"Is this where it happened? Where your dad fell?" Pearla asked. Annie's eyes opened wide and her hands covered her mouth as she nodded.

"Yes. I didn't want to look. I can't imagine. I don't even think I want to venture downstairs. The thought of my father falling and dying alone. It's so awful."

It was Pearla's turn to nod sadly. "I'm sorry," she said.

"There's another family room down there with a bar, and it leads outside. It was great for parties."

"Did your father spend much time downstairs after he moved back? It seems like everything he'd need is up on this floor, and these open stairs are really steep. No handrail either," Pearla said, hoping she wasn't pushing too hard, but wanting to lead Annie to her own conclusion.

She watched Annie's expression and could almost see the questions forming. Then Annie gasped. "Pearla, are you suggesting my father was pushed down the stairs?"

"Maybe?" Pearla's voice was tinged with hesitation, but she felt she had to tell Annie her whole theory. "Remember, your father had planned to change his will to stipulate the property couldn't be sold, but he died before he could."

Annie's eyes widened, and she wrapped her arms around herself as if to contain all the emotion she felt. It was then that they heard a vehicle pull into the driveway.

"Someone's coming," Annie said, panic rising. "We need to hide. I don't trust them."

Nor do I.

Annie took Pearla's hand and led her downstairs where they tucked themselves under the stairwell. The room was dark with the curtains closed, and they were not likely to be seen unless someone was specifically looking for them. They heard footfalls on the back deck and two male voices.

"It's Pete," Annie whispered. "I recognize his voice."

And as she strained to listen, Pearla's pulse raced when she heard the very distinct voice of Jack Morehouse. The exact conversation was difficult to decipher, but she feared the men entering the house. If they were dangerous, she and Annie would be trapped. Their best option was to stay still and hope the men would leave quickly. And then she heard the click of the lock, and the two men stepped into the kitchen. Pearla prayed they had no reason to come downstairs.

"Wanna cold one?" Pete said.

It's not even noon.

"You bet. We're about to cross the finish line," Jack said. "You'll look like a hero to your brothers. They might be pissed at first, but they'll come around. This is a much better deal than those two clowns came up with."

Pete responded with an unintelligible grunt. The next sound was of the refrigerator opening and then the cracking and fizzing of cans of beer.

"Hey, so what do you want me to do with the gun?" Jack asked.

"Why do you still have it? You shouldn't have anything that could tie us to the so-called *accidents*."

Pearla involuntarily shuddered at the sinister way Pete Junior said the word accidents.

"You asked me to get it from Martinez. I had to lift it from his trunk after his untimely death."

"Untimely, my ass. I'd say perfectly timed." They both laughed. "Well, I meant for you to dispose of it. Didn't we discuss sinking it in the pond?"

"Alright, I'll take care of it," Jack said. "It doesn't matter though; the killer's dead."

"True."

"So, when do we sign the papers? When's it official?"

"We're almost in the clear. I'll put the offer on the table, as if it just came up. They won't ask questions. Evan will be on board, and Seth will follow suit. We might have to offer Seth a little extra to make it final, but he'll fall in line. He always does. Then your uncle can write it up for the price we agreed to on paper, but pay us the rest on the side. We'll each get our extra bump. My brothers won't be any the wiser, and it's still a much better deal than they would have gotten."

"Cheers to that." The sounds of cans touching was followed by a loud belch and laughter.

"So, your sister is out of the picture and won't be an issue?"

"No. I think she's dead. She's been gone for years. I don't believe Seth actually got ahold of her. He's bluffing. Those texts are fake." Pete's voice exuded confidence.

"Good, that's good. Dude, this is really happening. We're gonna pull it off. Who cares about the protest? There's nothing they can do. Once it's sold, it's over. Everything will be according to the letter on paper."

Then, as if on cue, Annie's phone chirped, indicating she had a text. Pearla watched her fumble to shut off the volume.

"What the hell was that?" Pete's voice boomed. Pearla felt a wave of dizziness and struggled to stay standing and frozen to the spot.

"That was a phone. It came from downstairs. Someone's here," Jack said. "Pete, if you're double-crossing me, I will kill you. I mean it."

Pearla felt Annie squeeze her upper arm.

"Stay quiet," Annie hissed. Then, to Pearla's horror, Annie yelled out, "It's me, Pete. It's Annie. I'm here and I'm coming upstairs. I must have fallen asleep on the sofa down here; I was waiting for you to come home." Annie tramped up the stairs and joined the men in the kitchen.

"Whoa, hello little sis," Pete said, unable to disguise his utter confusion. Pearla wished she could see his expression, but was also scared for Annie's and her own safety. She held her phone under her hoodie, made sure the volume was off, and texted Sheriff Silva and Max.

"Bro, you look like you've seen a ghost," Jack said.

"I have. Annie, is it really you?"

"It's really me. In the flesh," Annie said in a calm and confident voice.

"But, I thought you were dead. I can't believe you're here," Pete said.

"Obviously, I'm not dead. Just avoiding you until I felt I couldn't anymore."

"Okay. So how long have you been in town?"

"Arrived yesterday. I came here earlier to wait for you. No one was home and I fell asleep. I woke up only when I heard my phone." Pearla wondered if they'd buy it.

"Yeah, right," Jack said. "This better not complicate things, Pete, because I'm not doing your dirty work again. You'll need to take care of this situation yourself."

"Shut up, you idiot," Pete warned.

"What is he talking about? What did you do, Pete? What exactly are you involved in?" Annie asked.

"I'm involved in taking control of our family's legacy. We are selling the property and getting what is rightfully ours. I suppose you'll need a cut now."

"Dad never wanted it sold, and you know it."

"That was only a silly sentimental dream. As if we were all going to live out our days here in his beloved Silvermist Point. Well, we're not. Sorry, dear old Dad." Pete and Jack both laughed.

"Um, excuse me. I don't know who you are, but would you mind leaving, please? I'd like to speak with my brother privately," Annie's voice exuded confidence. Pearla heard Jack cursing under his breath.

"Give me the keys, Pete, if you expect me to leave."

Pearla heard keys being tossed and the backdoor opening and closing. She didn't like the idea of Annie alone with her older brother and wondered what, if anything, she could use as a weapon if it came to that. It was dark, and even though her eyes had adjusted, it was still hard to see clearly. She peeked at her phone and was thankful to see a thumbs up from Max.

"Ok, good, we can talk privately. Pete, I don't know who that guy is, but he shouldn't be involved in our family's private business."

"Jack's trustworthy. I know what I'm doing."

"Do you, though? Does he know you pushed Dad down the stairs to his death?"

Pearla's stomach clenched. *Whoa. Why was Annie baiting him?*

"Oh, Annie, you know what happened. Dad lost his balance and fell down the stairs. Remember, you were too wrapped up in your own life to attend his funeral?"

"Okay, so listen, Pete. Cut the crap. I want in. I know I said I didn't want the money, but I do. It's complicated, but my circumstances have changed. I'm in some financial trouble of my own, so I won't judge you. You know I can keep secrets better than anyone. Seth and Evan don't need to know the details of whatever you've got going on here, but I do. I'm gonna grab a beer, and you can fill me in. Honestly, I'm glad you took care of Dad before he could change the will, or we'd all be screwed now."

Pearla heard the fridge open and the sound of another beer being popped.

"You should know, Annie, Dad had cancer. It was terminal, so he didn't have much time left. Going quickly was the best thing for him. He would have suffered otherwise."

Sure, so that justifies murdering him.

"Okay, enough about Dad. I'd rather not think about him right now. What is the 'dirty work' Jack was referring to? Maybe I can cover for you, like I used to."

What is she getting at?

"I don't need a cover. I'm not technically involved at all; that's the brilliance of it. Jack is an intelligent guy. We planned it out together. It seemed like a crazy scheme at first, I never thought we could pull it off, but here we are."

"Go on," Annie prompted.

"I may have suggested to one of our potential buyers a fool-proof way to take out his competition, and he may have done just that, on a promise he'd get the deal."

"How?" Annie pressed, and Pearla hoped she knew what she was doing.

"Modified paintball gun loaded with a camouflaged golf ball. This guy, Martinez, hit the victim dead center of his forehead."

Pearla could hear the bravado in his voice and picture the self-satisfied smirk on his face.

"Wow, that was brilliant," Annie praised. "So, you supplied the equipment?"

"Sure did. Guy was a crack shot. It was amazing, it came out of nowhere. You want to know the best part? The police have nothing. Tragic accident and no one's talking."

"What if this Martinez guy chooses to implicate you once he knows you and Jack double-crossed him?"

"He can't. He's dead. Jack ran him off the road and made it look like an accident."

"And what makes you so confident you can trust Jack? Or should we take him out too after the deal closes?"

"Annie, you'd do that?"

"There's so much you don't know about me, Pete. I'm not your innocent little sister. I've been up to a lot in the last seven years."

Annie sounded so convincing. A sliver of doubt crept into Pearla's mind and she wondered if this was an act. Was Annie playing her? Was she actually in danger, standing here trapped with no escape? She looked at her phone and saw that the thumbs up sign from Max was sent more than ten minutes ago. She knew Max would have immediately informed Sheriff Silva, whom Pearla had also texted. What was taking so long? Where were they?

With a shaky finger, she punched in 911. *I should have done that in the first place.* More urgent. She thought about sneaking out the sliding glass door into the yard and making a run for it. She'd need to cross the room and open the sliding door. If the door didn't slide easily or emitted any sound, she was cooked. If she made it out, she'd need to stay ahead of Pete and run for help. It wasn't worth the risk.

"Where are you going?" Annie's voice was suddenly very shrill and loud.

"Downstairs. Follow me," Pete said.

"No. Let's stay up here. It's really musty down there. I have allergies, and falling asleep on that moldy sofa didn't help." Too late.

Pearla heard the footsteps coming closer, and trembled as Pete flicked on the overhead light and descended the stairs. She had nowhere to hide. With the lights on, he would see her for sure. She pulled the strings of her black hoodie to tighten it and scrunched herself into the corner under the stairs. He might not see her if she stood still and he didn't look directly at her. And he wasn't expecting her to be there, so that was in her favor. Pearla prayed silently for her safety while wondering if and when Sheriff Silva would show up.

Pete stood in the middle of the room. All he'd have to do was slightly glance in her direction, and Pearla was toast.

"Remember all the fun times we had down here, all the parties? It was the best way to sneak in and out, too," Pete said.

"Are you forgetting how much younger than you I am, Pete? I was never included in your parties."

"Ah, right. Well, you're included now. Tell me more about what you've been up to. I'm curious."

"I started in Switzerland…" Annie recounted her past, but Pearla only half listened, hyper-focused on how she might escape. Pete's back was to Pearla. About two feet away was a pile of golf clubs. Pearla hoped she could pluck one off the top without making a sound or tumbling the rest. She had to try.

Slowly and painstakingly, she stepped closer to the precarious pile, then bent down to reach the club resting on the top. Focus. *This is just like pick-up sticks.* Her hand grabbed the metal shaft and she lifted in a quick motion. Pete must have sensed another person in the room. He spun around and was upon her in seconds.

Pearla swung the club in desperation, and missed completely, while Annie screamed in shock. "Who is this, Pete?"

Pete ripped the hood off Pearla's head. His eyes locked with hers. He recognized her.

"She runs the inn. I forgot her name," he spewed gruffly. "What are you doing in my house, lady?"

Pearla's throat went dry, and she couldn't answer.

"We should tie her up and figure out what to do. I'll hold her. You grab some rope," Annie directed as she grabbed Pearla tightly.

"Right." Pete's grip eased, letting Annie take over before crossing the room where he pulled open a drawer. Annie quickly flashed Pearla her phone. She had dialed 911. Pearla breathed out and relaxed a little, telling herself it would be any minute till help arrived.

"Lay down," Pete said as he shoved her to the floor then pressed into her back with his foot.

"Let me do it. I'll tie her up," Annie offered confidently.

"No, this needs to be tight, we can't have her getting away. I've got this. You can hold her down." Pete weaved the twine between Pearla's wrists and pulled it taut, securing it with a knot. He did the same to her ankles.

Pearla tried not to struggle, as the rough twine cut painfully into her skin. Finished with the task, Pete paced, exhaling in noisy bursts.

"This is just a wrinkle. We can take care of this." The arrogance in his voice made Pearla want to vomit.

"No," Annie said. "Wait for Jack. Make him do it. We don't need blood on our hands."

"Right, I'll message him. Jack can take care of the body. He can sink it in the pond, along with the gun."

I'm the body.

Chapter 26

Sheriff Silva

The group on the village green was larger than expected. Janice had worked her magic once again. Protestors held up handmade signs declaring their opposition to the sale and development of the Worley property. The signs read: Keep it Wild!, No Big Development!, and Donate the Land! On the stage, a microphone was set up, and villagers were taking turns voicing their disapproval. A white Channel Three news van hugged the curb near Mama's Pizza and the newscaster was circulating among the crowd to get the story. *This isn't likely to get violent.*

"Hey, how did you find out about the protest?" Rene asked one of the technical workers standing by the news van.

"Someone phoned it into the station as an anonymous tip. It was a light news day, so we took a drive out. It's a cute little town here. I've never been."

Rene was amazed at how so many people had no clue Silvermist Point existed. To be fair, he hadn't either, before he moved here. It was geographically close to Brookhaven, but most folks never ventured here. Silvermist was growing on Rene, and now that he'd served as sheriff for over a year, he thought of it as his home. While once he'd missed the fast action of the Los Angeles Police Department, now he relished this sleepy little town and all its quirky inhabitants.

Sheriff Rene Silva was at the protest to keep order and keep the peace, but he was also here to show his support. He agreed with his neighbors and did not want to see Silvermist grow into some type of tourist attraction. It was better to keep it small and quaint. As he scanned the crowd, his eyes landed on Max. She stood with Janice and Misty, the three of them chatting amicably and taking in the scene. Where was Pearla? He'd much prefer to see Pearla with her bright smile and charming unruly curls. He walked up to Max and greeted the three ladies with a smile.

"Well done, ladies. You put this together fast."

"That's thanks to Janice," Max said, giving credit where credit was due.

Sure enough, Janice had blasted out on the neighborhood app that residents should gather in the village square and protest the sale of the Worley property to big business. She'd also tipped off a local news reporter.

"Is that one of the Worley brothers up on the stage?" Janice pointed, squinting.

Rene watched Evan Worley lean down to take a microphone from one of the reporters and wondered how he would try to spin this to his advantage.

"If I can have your attention, please. I'm Evan Worley. I'm here to clear up any misconceptions and rumors spreading about the sale of my family's land."

"And what would those misconceptions be, sir?" a man shouted from the crowd.

"Well, you people have gotten the wrong impression. The land isn't zoned for big development. There's absolutely no reason for concern."

"The land was never to be sold at all," shouted another man. Whoops and cheers erupted from the crowd.

"That's Mr. O'Leary," Max said. "Pearla and I met him. He was a good friend of Pete Senior."

On the stage, Evan attempted to disagree with Mr. O'Leary, but O'Leary cut back in and was handed a second microphone from one of the reporters. He spoke again, his voice amplified, so all could hear.

"Now, young man, don't you forget I knew your dad. He meant for the land to stay in your family."

Rene chuckled that Mr. O'Leary referred to the middle-aged Evan Worley as 'young man.'

"Well, there's nothing in the will about that." Evan was trying to defend himself, but was gaining no points with the crowd.

"Oh, so he passed away before he could change it?" Mr. O'Leary shot back. "That's convenient for you boys then, I see."

The crowd cheered and clapped, then broke out in a chant. "No Sale, Keep it Wild!"

Rene felt his cell phone vibrate in his pocket. The text from Pearla read, "At Worley's. Come quick." When he looked up from his phone, Max was right next to him, tapping his arm.

"Pearla might be in trouble," her voice shaking.

"I know, she just sent me a message. She's at the Worley property."

"I'm coming with you," Max said, and they rushed to the police cruiser. Rene turned on the flashers as he made the quick drive. The front gate of the Worley property was swung wide open and a red Jeep was the only car he saw. He and Max jumped out.

"Max, stay in the cruiser until I check it out."

Max followed the directive and got back in the car. Rene called out Pearla's name and got no response. He walked further in and called out, "Police, show yourselves. This is private property and you are trespassing."

"I'm not trespassing, it's my property," a deep voice responded and Seth Worley appeared with his golf club. "What's up, Sheriff?"

Rene scanned the area, then asked, "Are you here alone?"

"Yes, what's this all about?"

"There was a report of suspicious activity," Rene improvised, then carefully studied Seth Worley's expression and noticed a twitch in his left eyebrow. "Do you know anything about that?"

Before Seth could answer, the emergency call came through on Rene's radio. Seth heard it.

"Hey, that's my family's house address. What's going on?"

Rene didn't owe him any explanation. He rushed back to the cruiser and drove full speed to the Worley house, hoping to arrive in time. The tension in the cruiser was palpable.

"Oh my gosh, it's the house Pearla meant, not the property." Max's voice was full of dread. "I thought she was going with Annie to the property. I stayed back because Annie trusted Pearla and I didn't want to interfere. Pearla was planning to meet me at the protest." Max choked up. "Rene, I can't lose her. I couldn't bear it."

Rene's job was to remain calm. "Max, don't think the worst. Nothing is going to happen to Pearla. No one is going to harm her. They'll have to go through me first, and I won't let that happen." *I cannot let that happen.*

They pulled into the driveway.

"That's Jack Morehouse's truck. I recognize it," Max said. There was another SUV in the driveway as well. Rene knew it would take some time for backup to arrive. He'd have to sort this himself.

Chapter 27

Pearla wondered how long it would take for Jack to return. Pete had called him immediately and said there was a situation they needed to deal with. He must not have been far, because before she knew it, he was back in the house and wrapping her in a tarp. When Jack bent down to pick up Pearla, intending to carry her out and throw her in the back of his truck, Annie swung a golf club and connected squarely with his skull, knocking him out cold.

Pete stood shocked as she tried to explain. "The police are coming. We're good, Pete. You can play the hero."

And as if on cue, Pearla heard the siren, followed by Rene's voice on the bullhorn, "Police, come out with your hands up." The rest was a blur as Annie ran upstairs and out the front door while Pete attempted to elude capture and slip out the back. Pearla lay helpless and waiting, tied up and unable to move, while Jack remained unconscious a few feet away.

Rene stormed downstairs, gun drawn and pointed at Jack. He switched to his taser and delivered a nice shock to Jack, just to make certain he was indeed incapacitated. Then, he deftly untied Pearla's wrists and ankles and insisted she be checked out by paramedics.

Pearla wasn't sure if she was imagining it, but he seemed very emotional, even giving her a tight hug and saying, "Thank God you're safe."

When Jack regained consciousness, he found himself in custody. Pete was caught quickly. He had not made it far into the woods and was taken down by a blast from the sheriff's taser. With the recorded conversations admitting to their actions and the physical evidence, Pearla was confident both men would spend a fair amount of time behind bars.

Chapter 28

Saturday
Max

Max and Pearla each sprawled in Adirondack chairs by the fire pit, reflecting on another satisfactory week of living at and managing the Snowy Plover Inn. It was still early, and they balanced their mugs of coffee on the wide arms of the chairs. Butters was prowling nearby, occasionally checking in by rubbing his body against their legs and asking for pets.

"If it wasn't for the drama of the two murders, I'd say we had yet another great week," Pearla quipped.

Max laughed, but her voice grew serious. "I'm so grateful Sheriff Silva came to the rescue in time. I can't live without you."

"Pete wouldn't have done it. He's not capable. That guy was too chicken to do anything himself," Pearla's voice was confident, but Max knew it could have ended badly.

Butters paused mid-purr, the fur on his spine stood straight up and his tail puffed into a feather duster.

"What's up, Butty?" Max asked. Then they heard the jingle of the tags fastened to Chief's collar, and his excited barks once he saw his cat friend.

"Good morning, ladies," Tyne called.

Max turned, a smile lighting her whole face in the slanted sunlight. "Hey, come join us," she said.

"I was hoping you'd ask. I already helped myself to coffee in the living room. Thank God you're okay, Pearla. That could've gone sideways quickly."

"I'm fine," Pearla said, obviously trying to downplay what had been a close call.

"Guests checking out today?" Tyne changed the subject.

"Yes, except for Annie. She's staying on for the week and doesn't want to stay in the Worley house alone. Plus, we've bonded a bit after yesterday's ordeal," Pearla said.

As Tyne settled himself into a chair and stretched out his legs, Max noticed he was wearing his flip-flops and asked, "Are you headed to the shore after this?"

"Yup, I want to let Chief get in a run. If you two are free, I thought we could look for the cave. It's low tide."

"Oh, I'd love to," Max said without hesitation.

"Me too, but Emma called in sick so I'm freshening the rooms and getting set for the new guest check-ins. Full house again next week, thankfully. You two go ahead without me. Just remember where the cave is, Max, so you can show Char and me."

Pearla looked at Max directly and gave her a wide-eyed,

innocent stare. It confirmed Max's suspicion that Pearla was purposely bowing out. She was providing Max with some alone time with Tyne, even though Max had tried to make it abundantly clear that yes, even though Tyne was gorgeous, friendly, kind, and single, she was not looking to get involved with anyone romantically.

Friendship is all I can handle at this point in my life.

After a few more minutes of chatting about yesterday's events, Pearla stood and offered to take their mugs back inside.

"Let's go," Tyne said, and they started on the wood-chipped path to the shore. Once at the sand line, they kicked off their flip-flops and left them on a piece of driftwood before crossing the sand to the edge of the shore. Tyne kept Chief on his leash. There still might be Snowy Plovers nesting in the grassy dunes and they wouldn't want to disturb them. Max rolled her jeans to her knees, and Tyne did the same before they walked on the wet sand with the shallow waves lapping at their feet.

* * *

Max and Tyne walked in comfortable silence, and Max couldn't help but wonder what he was thinking about. He stooped to grab a piece of sea glass, then held the quarter-sized, milky white piece up to the light to inspect it.

"Good enough?" he asked.

"Pearla is the collector, more than I am, but it looks pretty good to me. Well-seasoned, no rough edges, good curve. Keeper."

Tyne held it out to her, then dropped it in her palm.

"Thanks." Max rubbed it between her fingers before

shoving it in her back pocket. They walked on, and she could feel in her bones they were near the cave. It was an odd sensation.

Tyne was walking close to the face of the cliff. "This is it," he shouted victoriously after pulling back some overgrown bushes. He pointed. "Just up ahead is the trail down from the bluff. The one my friends and I used to take as kids."

"I think you're right. I remember when Char and I first found it, it was totally camouflaged and that was ... a long time ago." Max had almost said thirty-nine years ago, but thought better of it. She still marveled at how so much time had passed.

"Follow me if you're brave enough," Tyne dared. He turned on his phone flashlight and headed in with Chief.

Max remembered Char's fear of bats and desperately hoped there were none living in the cave. She flicked on her flashlight and mentally prepared to follow Tyne in.

"No bats," he called out, just as Max had done for Char years ago. Max pushed her anxiety aside and entered the cave, and once inside, she knew this was the very same one she and Char had found on Christmas Eve when they were thirteen.

"Hey, when Char and I were here last, we found a journal in a plastic bag."

"I know it," Tyne said, then pointed at the cave wall. "My initials."

Max was surprised to see TB written on the wall in what looked like soot. How had it been so perfectly preserved after all these years?

"Char and I didn't put our initials on the wall, but we left a message in the book."

Tyne was already pulling the old zipper-top plastic bag out of a cubby hole in the wall. He held it up. "This?" he asked and removed it from the bag.

"Yes, we were planning to come to the meeting that summer, but we didn't make it back."

"I know you didn't. I'm having a super weird feeling of *déjà vu* right now. It's like my teen years are all flooding back to me. I always wondered who left the message in the book, who those initials belonged to."

Max nodded; she felt it too.

"How surreal that we've both stood in this exact place, but never knew each other," she said, as goosebumps rose on her arms, making her shiver.

"I'm glad we know each other now." He was standing very close and Max grappled with all the emotions she was feeling. All she could say was, "Me too." Tyne gently took her hand.

"If I remember, there was a smaller cavern back here." He led her into the area that was only really big enough for one person.

Max let go of his hand, and Tyne turned so they were face to face in the small space. Max was grateful for the low light of the flashlight. Her face burned and was likely all kinds of red.

"I'm sorry. I didn't mean to make you uncomfortable."

Oh, no, I don't want him to think that. Why am I so awkward? "You're not, it's just I…"

Thankfully, Tyne interrupted. "Maxine Egan, you are a beautiful woman. I can't tell you how happy it has made me that you moved to Silvermist Point. I love spending time with you. And Pearla, too. Would I like to date you at some point, if you were interested? Yes, yes, I would. But

I'm perfectly content to stay as friends. I'm sure we would have been friends if we'd met years ago." He laughed a little. "I think I just said the quiet part out loud. I might be blushing."

Max laughed too and felt relief flood through her entire body. "Tyne, the last thing I want is for us to *not* be friends. You might be my favorite person in Silvermist Point." Max couldn't see very well, but she was sure Tyne was smiling, same as her.

"I'll take that. You might be mine, too," Tyne said.

"Pearla and I are considering letting you join our amateur crime fighting team."

"I thought I was already on the team. Sheesh, what do I have to do to earn my place? Is there some sort of application process? Who is my competition?"

"Oh, I'll let you know," Max teased.

I appreciate your taking the time to read *Tee Time Tragedy at the Snowy Plover Inn*. If you enjoyed it please tell your friends, and I would be so grateful if you would consider posting a review. Word of mouth is an author's best friend, and very much appreciated.
Thank you,

Deanna Nese

* * *

Up Next in This Series!
Fans and Felonies at the Snowy Plover Inn
Book Three, Snowy Plover Inn Cozy Mystery Series

It's spring. There's a festival coming to the village and the Snowy Plover Inn is fully booked. This is just the event to put Silvermist Point on the map, but not everyone in the village welcomes the influx of tourists. One of the bands is an internet sensation with scores of fans crushing on the bandmates. During the concert, fans are in high spirits, until one enthusiastic groupie who happens to be lodging at the Snowy Plover Inn, turns up dead. Was there something in her margarita?

Acknowledgements

As always, I thank my family. My wonderful husband, Sam, and my children, Dylan and Clara, who always encourage me to persevere with my writing. Your support means everything to me. Thank you to my readers, it's beyond wonderful to hear from you and to have actual fans. Deepest thanks go out to: Nicole O'Meara, for trading pages with me and giving me valuable feedback; Phyllisanne Maguire for her critique and support all along the way. At Secret Staircase Books, I am grateful to my publishing team: Stephanie Dewey, Sandra Anderson, Susan Gross, Isobel Tamney, Paula Webb, Eve Osbourne, and Gabi Hoffknecht for making the story shine.

Thank you, God, for this gift you have given me, and for allowing me to share it with the world.

Books in the Snowy Plover Inn series:

Checked Out at the Snowy Plover Inn
Christmas at the Snowy Plover Inn (a holiday novella)
Tee Time Tragedy at the Snowy Plover Inn

**Sign up for Deanna's newsletter and get a
free book!
deannanese.com**

Deanna Nese published three novels in various genres before settling into cozy mysteries. She has published short stories in Typishly and the VC Reporter. Her love of writing and reading runs deep. She teaches middle schoolers English and History, enjoys outdoor activities, traveling, and spending time with her family. She is a member of the Crime Writers Association and West Coast Christian Writers.

Find her at these online sites:
Facebook Deanna Nese: Author
Substack. @deannanese1
Instagram @deannaneseauthor
Twitter @deanna_nese
Pinterest: neseteach